Daycare Dangers

MariaLisa deMora

First Published 2026

ISBN 13: 978-1-946738-96-7

DEDICATION

"Me: Did you fart? Son: Sorry, mom. When I'm nervous I fart." ~ Winter Travers

For all parents of creative and cantankerous kids: You're doing a great job!

Contents

ACKNOWLEDGMENTS

Hiya, everyone.

There's something to be said about finalizing an idea that started over eight years ago, and finding that it's still a viable project. Feels pretty darn good!

Huge thanks to Becky Johnson and her crew at Hot Tree Edits. I've enjoyed working with Kristen, Kim, and everyone else on this venture.

To my readers, if you've been around for a while, you know that I'm not faithful to any given genre. I'm liable to go after them all! This book opens a new one for me, in cozy mysteries. This book feels like the first of a series, so here's hoping y'all like the idea.

Woofully yours,
~ML

Daycare Dangers

In the idyllic small town of Willow Creek, Sunnybrook Cottage Daycare is a haven of laughter, glitter, and innocent secrets...until one child's whispers turn deadly.

Theresa Daye loves her life running the colorful daycare, capturing hilarious kid quips on her popular blog, and sharing hugs with her pint-sized charges. But when a cryptic email echoes a private conversation from the playroom, quoting a shy girl's eerie mantra, "smart people always come out on top," Theresa's world of rainbow doors and nap-time stories unravels into a chilling maze of hidden dangers.

As anonymous threats escalate, a blurry photo of a child's drawing arrives, revealing secrets that point to a web of corporate intrigue, a suspicious uncle, and a cold-case murder lurking closer than the playground fence. With the help of a charming librarian and her loyal assistant, Theresa must navigate shadowy watchers, courtroom dramas, and her own budding romance, all while protecting the little ones who trust her most.

But in a place where monsters hide behind finger-paint smiles, can Theresa uncover the truth before the next "quip" becomes a cry for help?

Daycare Danger is a heartwarming cozy mystery brimming with small-town charm, adorable antics, and edge-of-your-cot suspense. Wall Street Journal and USA Today bestselling author MariaLisa deMora delivers a tale where the stakes are as high as a tire swing—and the exits lead to justice.

Chapter One

Theresa Daye balanced her travel mug in one hand and the ring of keys in the other, the brass jangling like wind chimes as she approached the rainbow-painted front door of Sunnybrook Cottage Daycare.

The paint on the daycare's front and back doors was her own handiwork from three years ago, on a crazy whim after a particularly trying week of spilled paint and glitter glue disasters. Over time, the colors had faded a little under the Willow Creek sun, but they still made the old Victorian cottage look like a storybook illustration come to life.

And Theresa still loved it.

Most mornings, she'd pause with her forehead against the door, whispering the same silly prayer she'd made up the first week she owned the place: "Let today be the day no one cries before nine, no one bites, and nobody mistakes glitter for a food group. Amen."

Today, before she could slide the key into the lock, a small tornado in dinosaur pajamas launched itself at her left leg.

"Miss T! You're late!" Milo announced loudly, his voice muffled against her jeans. At four, the son of her assistant manager had the grip strength of a baby koala and the dramatic timing of a Shakespearean actor. "Back door's been open all morning."

Theresa laughed, steadying herself with a hand on the doorframe. "It's seven twenty-nine, buddy. I'm actually one minute early to open the front door."

Milo tilted his head, considering this, then tightened his hold. "Still late for hugs."

She couldn't argue with that logic. Setting her mug on the porch railing, she crouched to return the embrace, inhaling the familiar scent of baby shampoo and graham crackers that clung to every child in her care. Milo's curls tickled her cheek as he planted a sticky kiss on her nose.

"Better?" she asked.

"Much." He released her leg but kept one small hand fisted in her sweater as she finally unlocked the door.

The cottage smelled of lemon polish and yesterday's sculpting clay. Theresa flicked on the lights, revealing the open floor plan she'd fought the zoning board for. She smiled as she took in the cozy circle-time rug in primary colors, low tables surrounded by pint-sized chairs, and a reading nook piled with cushions and board books. The walls were a gallery of finger-paint masterpieces and two construction-paper turkeys that had survived last November's craft apocalypse.

Milo made a beeline for the block corner, already narrating an elaborate battle between plastic dinosaurs. Theresa smiled and moved to the kitchenette, where Mia Torres was wrestling with the industrial coffee maker like it had personally offended her.

"Morning, sunshine," Mia said without looking up. At twenty-eight, her assistant manager had the energy of someone who'd mainlined espresso and the sarcasm of someone who'd been awake since five. Her dark hair was twisted into a knot held together by what appeared to be a crayon. "Tell me you brought the good creamer."

"French vanilla, as requested." Theresa set the bottle on the counter. "Also, Milo met me out front and has decided I'm late for hugs. I think that's going to be his new thing."

"Kids latch onto the weirdest hills to die on." Mia finally coaxed the machine into gurgling obedience. "I saw Mrs. Hargrove's already circling the parking lot like a shark. I swear that woman times her arrivals with a stopwatch."

Theresa groaned. Mrs. Hargrove was the local president of the PTA, the self-appointed guardian of childhood nutrition, and a perpetual thorn in her side. The woman was also the reason the cottage had a strict "no nuts, no gluten, no joy" policy taped to the fridge.

As if summoned by the mention of her name, the front door chimed. Mrs. Hargrove swept in, trailing the scent of expensive perfume and judgment. She did not simply drop off a sweet six-year-old Landon and leave.

First, she performed what Theresa and Mia privately called the "Full Audit."

The audit always began with Landon's bento box inspection. Every day it was the same. She opened each silicone compartment as if expecting to discover a rogue stowaway peanut, regardless that it had been packed at her house.

The audit continued with a slow circuit of the room while narrating her findings aloud. "I see the water table still has that green tint. Have you tested for bacteria?" And it culminated in a ten-minute lecture on the developmental risks of allowing screen time before 9:00 a.m. because "what happens in the morning sets the course for all day," and shorter attention and lax morals wouldn't be accepted for her son. Of course not.

All of this was delivered while Landon stood silently at her side, clutching his stainless steel briefcase of snacks like a tiny bodyguard.

"Theresa," Mrs. Hargrove said, managing to make the declaration sound like an accusation. "I need to bring you up to speed. Landon has a new dietary restriction. His naturopath says quinoa is inflammatory."

Theresa plastered on her professional smile. "Noted. We'll make sure any snacks are quinoa-free."

Mrs. Hargrove's eyes narrowed as though she sensed the buried sarcasm in Theresa's response, then scanned the room a final time, clearly expecting to find contraband grains hidden in the block bin.

Satisfied for the moment, she kissed Landon's forehead, more air than contact, and departed with a rustle of dry-clean-only fabrics.

When Mrs. Hargrove finally left, Mia appeared at Theresa's elbow holding two mugs like peace offerings.

"I put holy water in yours," she whispered. "And a shot of whiskey."

Theresa laughed until she snorted, which got Mia started with a fit of the giggles. Theresa was gasping for breath by the time they'd stopped. "Oh, Mia, I needed that laugh. Thank you. I approve the application of holy water. Maybe we should do that every day?"

"Maybe." Mia turned back to the coffee maker.

The rest of the morning unfolded in its familiar rhythm. Children arrived in waves, some bounding in and some dragged by parents chronically running late for work. Theresa greeted each by name, accepting sticky fingers and from-home artwork that would later be proudly displayed on the "Parent Pickup Wall of Fame."

By eight thirty, every cubby was occupied, every coat hung backward because the children insisted sleeves were wings. Theresa rang the brass bell above the circle-time rug, giving it three clear chimes, and twelve bodies arranged themselves in something resembling a circle.

"Good morning, friends!" she sang.

"Good morning, Miss T!" they chorused, some shouting, some whispering, and Milo roaring like a dinosaur.

"Who can tell me what the weather is today?"

Hands shot up. Priya Delgado waved so hard she nearly levitated.

"Priya?"

"It's rainbow weather," she declared. "Because the sun is shiny and my feelings are happy."

Theresa's heart did a cartwheel. "Perfect. Rainbow weather it is."

Then came the part she loved second best in the whole day: the pledge. She stood, hand over heart, and the children mirrored her, twelve small hands slamming over twelve small hearts.

"I pledge allegiance to the playroom rules of Sunnybrook Cottage Daycare, to be kind, to be safe, to be me, with glitter and blocks for all."

Milo added an enthusiastic "Rawr!" at the end, which everyone had decided counted as an amen.

She settled all her charges with paper and crayons, watching to see they were all happily drawing their favorite animal. Even Milo was studiously bent over his paper, the green scrawl of color roughly resembling the outline of a T-Rex.

Morning snack prep had to happen now. Theresa sliced apples with the precision of a sushi chef while Mia portioned goldfish crackers into paper cups.

The children washed their hands at the child-sized sink, singing the alphabet song twice through because "that's what the germs like."

Priya, six going on sixty, raised her hand during cleanup. "Miss T, my goldfish died."

Theresa paused, apple slice halfway to her mouth. "I'm so sorry, sweetie. What was his name?"

"Mr. Bubbles the Third. He forgot how to swim and just floated at the top like a crouton."

Now it was Mia's turn to snort so hard she inhaled a goldfish.

Theresa bit back a laugh, pulling out her phone to jot the quote in her notes app. It would be *Kid Quips* blog gold.

Messy art time was Theresa's true favorite thing of the day. The kids loved it too.

The art corner always turned into controlled chaos, paint smocks fluttering like superhero capes as the children attacked blank paper with watercolors. Most of the children slapped paint with abandon, mixing colors and palettes unrestrained. Milo constructed a square block tower of alternating colors that he insisted was a volcano hospital. Landon Hargrove used only primary colors and arranged his dots in perfect grids.

Emily Johnson, the newest addition to their little family, worked quietly at the end table. She was eight years old and still adjusting after moving to Willow Creek. She'd come here to live with her uncle after a horrific accident that took both of her parents from her, and for her art, she favored intricate mazes drawn in black ink. Even now, she had rejected crayons, markers, and paint. Instead, she worked with a single black gel pen she had brought from home in a plastic pencil case decorated with tiny unicorns.

Theresa drifted closer, pretending to refill glue sticks.

The paper was almost filled now with corridor after corridor, some wide, some so narrow and concentrated the ink had bled through the paper. Dead ends were marked with tiny, meticulous X's. At the very center was a stick figure with long hair and a triangle dress—clearly Emily herself, arms raised. Theresa couldn't tell if the figure was cheering or screaming.

She crouched. "That's incredible, Em. It's like a whole world."

Emily didn't look up. "It's a secret world."

"Are you in there?"

A pause. Then the smallest nod.

Theresa waited, giving the silence room to breathe.

"Uncle Victor says smart people always come out on top," Emily whispered again, so softly Theresa almost missed it.

"He sounds like a smart guy."

"Yeah." Emily's agreement was lackluster.

Theresa's heart did a little flip, part pride at the trust, part ache for whatever weight an eight-year-old carried that required such wisdom. She made a mental note to anonymize the quote for tonight's blog post.

Still, the blunt phrase lodged like a burr under Theresa's ribs. She filed it away with the same mental tag she used for bite incidents and allergic reactions. *Watch. Listen. Protect.*

The day blurred on. Outdoor playtime in the fenced backyard, where the slide had been dubbed "Mount Doom" by the older kids. Lunch was peanut-free sunbutter sandwiches and carrot sticks that inevitably ended up in someone's hair.

Then it was naptime, when the cottage fell into a hush broken only by the soft symphony of breathing and the occasional snore from Milo, who slept with one arm flung over his stuffed triceratops.

At two thirty, the library van pulled up for story hour. Alex Reed stepped out, arms full of picture books and a smile that always made Theresa's stomach perform Olympic gymnastics.

"Special delivery," he announced, holding up *The Day the Crayons Quit.*

His niece Lily, five and fearless, barreled past Theresa to tackle his legs.

"Hi, Uncle Alex!" She released him and looked back at me. "Miss T, Uncle Alex says you're his favorite grown-up!"

Alex's ears went pink. "I said she runs her daycare like a library, filled with organized chaos."

"Same thing," Theresa teased, taking the book. Their fingers brushed, and she felt the spark all the way to her toes.

Story hour was a hit, as always. Alex had a gift for voices, and his crayon impressions had even Mrs. Hargrove's Landon giggling without shame. When the last page turned, the children begged for one more, but the clock declared it was nearly pickup time.

"Thank you, Alex. The kids will never be happy with my voices again."

Lily laughed, and Alex blushed and dipped his chin. "I'm available anytime you need, Theresa. All you have to do is call."

A couple of minutes later, goodbye waves were exchanged and Theresa had escaped back to the kitchen. She opened the freezer door and stood there for a moment, letting her own flush dissipate.

Parents trickled in. Hugs were exchanged, artwork distributed, and reminders given about tomorrow's show-and-tell to include "nothing breathing or recently breathing." By six o'clock, the cottage was quiet again, toys tidied, floors swept of rogue glitter. Mia and Milo strolled out the back door, another pair of goodbye waves exchanged.

Theresa locked up and drove the short distance to where her apartment above the hardware store waited. She loved the little apartment; it was her sanctuary. The space was small but hers. From her overflowing bookshelves, a kitchenette that smelled of vanilla candles, and a desk overlooking Main Street, it was hard to pick out her favorite aspect.

She kicked off her shoes, changed into leggings and an oversized sweater, and brewed a tasty herbal tea in her preferred mug, the one with *World's Okayest Daycare Manager* in chipped letters.

Dinner was leftover lasagna and the latest episode of a baking show she pretended not to be obsessed with. Then, absolutely the best part of her nightly ritual, she opened her laptop to the *Kid Quips* dashboard.

Kid Quips had started as a nightly email she sent to cousins and friends, highlighting one hilarious saying after another from the kids. Then a friend was traveling overseas and wouldn't have access to her email for the duration, so Theresa had tackled learning the ins and outs of blogging software. Now, *Kids Quips* was one of her favorite times of the day that wasn't interacting directly with the kiddos.

Tonight's post was titled *Croutons and Other Aquatic Mysteries*. She typed up Priya's goldfish quote, swapping names and details to protect the innocent. Then she added a cartoon illustration she'd commissioned over lunch from a local art student and hit Publish.

The comments rolled in immediately, from heart emojis, laughing emojis, to the occasional "My kid said the exact same thing!" Tips trickled into her digital wallet with $3 here, $5 there. Enough to cover the electric bill and maybe a new box of crayons.

She was about to close the laptop when a new email notification pinged. The sender was a generic-looking free email address from gotmail.com, *playroomwatcher88*. Subject line: *Important Question*.

Odd, I don't usually get email from the blog. Wonder how they got this address. She used it to contact families often, but as far as she could remember, she didn't have a publicly listed address on the blog.

Theresa clicked on the message.

"The girl who 'always comes out on top.' I need you to tell me her name. Or the next story won't be funny."

Her tea went cold, untouched. The words glowed on the screen, innocuous and chilling. She reread them twice, three times. A prank? Some internet troll who'd taken the blog's anonymity challenge too far?

Theresa screenshotted the message, her pulse thudding in her ears. She considered deleting it, blocking the sender, pretending it never happened.

Instead, she saved it to a new folder labeled *WEIRD*.

Because in her line of work, weird was usually just a kid mistaking the cat for a hat.

But something about the phrasing, and the way it so closely echoed Emily's private whisper, lodged under her skin like a splinter.

She closed the laptop, drew her knees to her chest, and stared out the window at Willow Creek's quiet streets. Somewhere below, a car door slammed. Footsteps echoed on the sidewalk.

Theresa told herself the email was nothing.

She almost believed it.

Chapter Two

Theresa's alarm chirped at six fifteen, but she'd already been awake for twenty minutes, staring at the ceiling fan's lazy rotation. The email from *playroomwatcher88* had burrowed into her dreams, filling them with faceless figures chasing her through endless mazes while children's laughter echoed from every corner. She rolled out of bed, padded to the kitchenette, and brewed coffee strong enough to wake the dead.

By seven twenty, she was back at Sunnybrook Cottage, unlocking the rainbow door with a determined click.

Mia arrived minutes later, juggling a tray of coffees and a bakery bag. "Peace offering," she said, handing Theresa a croissant. "Figured we needed a carb reward after yesterday's Hargrove ambush."

Milo greeted her with his usual leg hug, but today he added a new twist, a plastic stethoscope draped around his neck.

"I'm Doctor Dinosaur now," he informed her solemnly. "You have glitter in your lungs."

Theresa coughed theatrically. "Good thing you're here to save me."

The morning routine flowed smoother than yesterday. Most parents were less harried, and their children less clingy.

Emily arrived at eight sharp, dropped off by a man in a charcoal suit who barely paused long enough to sign the clipboard. Her uncle Her guardian. Victor Johnson's signature was a sharp slash of ink, all angles and impatience. Same as every day.

Except today he lingered half a second longer.

Emily clutched her spiral notebook to her chest like armor. Victor crouched awkwardly, knees cracking loud enough for Theresa to hear, and said something that made Emily's shoulders curl inward.

Theresa stepped forward instinctively. "Morning, Mr. Johnson! Emily, Priya saved you a spot at the puzzle table."

Victor straightened, expression smoothing into polite blankness. "She knows where to find me if she needs anything." A pause, then, almost too soft to hear: "Remember what we talked about, Em. Smart girls come out on top."

He was gone before Theresa could respond.

Emily lingered by the coat hooks, still clutching her notebook covered in unicorn stickers.

"Morning, Em," Theresa said softly. "Want to hang your jacket with the others?"

Emily nodded but didn't move. Her eyes, a storm-cloud shade of gray, scanned the room as if cataloging exits. Finally, she slipped the notebook into her cubby, hung up her jacket, and joined the others on the circle-time rug.

Story time was *Where the Wild Things Are*. Theresa did the voices, aiming at an Alex-worthy portrayal of Max's mother, a weary alto, while the Wild Things were a chorus of growls and giggles. Emily sat cross-legged at the edge, lips moving silently as if memorizing the pages. When Theresa reached the part where Max sails home, after the story was done, Emily leaned over and whispered, "Uncle Victor says if you're smart, you always come out on top."

Theresa's heart stuttered. Same phrase as yesterday, delivered with the gravity of a secret oath. She tucked a loose strand of Emily's hair behind her ear. "I remember. That's a good lesson. Want to draw it later?"

Emily's nod was barely perceptible.

Art time in the back corner became maze central. Emily had commandeered a table of her own, tongue peeking from the corner of her mouth as she drew with her black gel pen. The design was more complex than yesterday's. It was comprised of layer upon layer of corridors, dead ends marked with tiny *X*'s, a single stick figure at the heart of it all. Theresa snapped a discreet photo for the blog, quickly cropping out Emily's face and any identifying details.

Lunch was grilled cheese sandwiches cut into star shapes, with tomato soup that inevitably ended up on someone's sleeve. Naptime brought the usual negotiations. Today, Milo insisted Doctor Dinosaur needed to check pulses before lights-out. Theresa obliged, letting him press the stethoscope to her wrist after she dimmed the lamps.

Emily didn't sleep. She lay on her cot staring at the ceiling, fingers tracing invisible patterns in the air. Theresa pretended not to notice, but her stomach knotted, unease riding up her spine. Whatever secrets Emily was keeping, they weren't conducive to healing rest.

Pickup was a whirlwind. Mrs. Hargrove arrived early again, this time armed with a printed article to expand on her obsession about the dangers of screen time. "Landon must retain his intellectual prowess and not be dumbed down by—" She leaned in and whispered the next bit. "—cartoons."

"The good thing is, we only do cartoons one day a week, and that's for just thirty minutes. So if he's being exposed to electronic entertainment, it's not happening at daycare."

Not swayed by facts, Mrs. Hargrove continued on in the same vein for another five minutes. Theresa was sure to nod in all the right places, all while mentally calculating how many goldfish crackers equaled a serving of vegetables.

By the end of pickup time, the cottage had emptied. Theresa locked up and drove the five blocks to Willow Creek Public Library, a red-brick building with gargoyles that looked perpetually surprised. The library was half-full of mostly seniors returning large-print romances and teenagers pretending to study while scrolling on social media.

Alex was behind the circulation desk, scanning a stack of board books. His hair was more tousled than yesterday, as if he'd been running his hands through it. When he spotted Theresa, his smile lit the room brighter than the fluorescent lights.

"Don't tell me. You've decided you need a research partner," he said, sliding a cart of returns aside. "Lily's still talking about your Wild Things impression. I'm under strict orders to bring *Goodnight Gorilla* next time."

Theresa laughed. "Deal. But first, I need help with something less gorilla related. I have a little girl who's quoted the same 'lesson' two days in a row to me, and I want to see if it has a meaning. 'If you're smart, you always come out on top.'"

Alex frowned. "'If you're smart, you always come out on top'? In what context? How do we even make sense of that phrase?" The frown faded into a smile. Not full wattage, but close enough for Theresa's heart to skip a beat. "Ah. This is for the blog, isn't it? All right, I'll be your partner in crime. Follow me." He led the way to the reference section, a quiet alcove smelling of old paper and lemon furniture pol sh. Alex pulled a volume of idioms from the shelf, *The Oxford Dictionary of Phrase and Fable.*

"'Come out on top,'" he read aloud, flipping pages. "Originated in boxing, late nineteenth century. Means to emerge victorious despite odds. Also used in gambling—poker, specifically."

Theresa chewed her lip. "Any darker connotations?"

Alex's brow furrowed. He exchanged the book for a legal dictionary. "In crim nal law, it can refer to someone avoiding conviction. 'Coming out on top' of a plea deal, for example."

A chill skittered down Theresa's spine. She told him about the email, omitting the sender's handle but quoting it verbatim. Alex's expression shifted from curious to concerned.

"Could be a coincidence," he said, but his tone lacked conviction. "Still, maybe change your blog's privacy settings. At least you can control the narrative there, by requiring approval for comments."

Theresa nodded, but her mind was already racing. Victor Johnson's sharp signature. Emily's mazes. The phrase repeated like a mantra.

They spent another hour digging through old newspaper archives on microfilm, a dusty volume on child psychology. When Alex's knee brushed hers under the table, neither moved away. When Alex stretched and his back cracked, Theresa realized they'd been there for two hours.

"Coffee?" Alex asked as they stepped into the evening air. "That café on Maple does a killer lavender latte."

"Tempting," Theresa said, "but I've got a blog post to write. Rain check?"

"Anytime." He hesitated, then added with a wry version of his dialed-back smile, "Text me if anything else weird pops up, okay? I know people who know people."

She watched him walk to his truck, a dented blue pickup with a *Read More Books* bumper sticker. Something warm unfurled in her chest, chasing away the chill from earlier.

Back at her apartment, Theresa uploaded the maze photo to *Kid Quips*. She titled it *Maze Master (age 8)*. The caption was "Some kids build castles. This one builds labyrinths. When I asked what happens if you get lost, she said, 'Smart people always come out on top.' Out here pondering life choices and whether I'd survive the Minotaur."

She hit Publish and watched the likes climb—500, 1,000, 2,000 in under an hour. Tips pinged in, from $5, to $10, and a generous $20 from *AnonymousBookworm*. By nine o'clock, she'd made $47. Enough for a new set of washable markers and maybe a pizza night.

Theresa was rinsing her chamomile mug when the second email arrived from playroomwatcher88@gotmail.com.

The subject line was *Nice Try*.

"Cute maze. But some doors should stay closed."

Attached was a blurry photo. As she studied it, Theresa's breath caught in her chest. It was Emily's drawing, the exact one from today, complete with the tiny *X*'s and the stick figure. But the crop was wrong. Theresa had cut off the bottom third to protect privacy. This version showed the full page, including Emily's name scrawled in the corner in purple marker.

She looked at the image a second time, realizing that it wasn't her photo. Hers had originally included Emily's face, which she'd then cropped out. This photo was of the actual drawing. The background was too blurry to decide definitively where the image may have been taken. She didn't remember if Emily had taken the maze home with her today or not.

Theresa opened her security software and found no alerts. No one had gone into the daycare since she'd closed up shop.

Her hands shook as she forwarded the email to herself from her phone, then deleted it from her inbox. She considered calling the police, but what would she say? *"Someone sent me a creepy email about a child's drawing"?* Officer Daniels would pat her on the head and tell her to lock her doors.

Instead, she opened her blog's settings and changed her passwords, then switched the comments to moderated. Then she paced.

Later in the evening, restless energy propelled her to the window. She leaned against the frame, looking down on a quiet Main Street, the thoroughfare dimly lit by only the glow of the pharmacy sign and the occasional car. But across the street, half hidden in the shadow of the hobby store, sat a black SUV. Tinted windows, no plates visible. It had been at the cottage when Victor dropped Emily off this morning. But it was not his vehicle. Theresa was sure of it.

She grabbed her phone, zoomed in, and snapped a photo of a blank license frame. The SUV's engine hummed to life. Headlights flared, blinding her for a second. Then it pulled away slowly, tires crunching over gravel, disappearing around the corner toward the highway. The back license frame was also blank, and she hadn't seen a paper license taped on the windows.

Theresa stood frozen, curtain clutched in her fist. The apartment felt too small, the walls pressing in. She double-checked the deadbolt, then the window locks.

Her phone buzzed with a text from Alex.

Just checking in. All okay?

She stared at the message, then at the empty street below.

Yeah, all is well, she typed. *But maybe dinner soon? I could use a friend.*

His reply was instant: *Name the time and place. Or I will. :)*

Theresa set the phone down and opened her laptop again. The blog's dashboard showed 2,147 likes now. A new comment waited for approval.

"Ask Maze Girl what Daddy did in the basement."

She deleted it, hands trembling. Then she opened a new document and titled it "Emily Johnson – Notes."

"Black SUV. No plates. 7:58 a.m. at drop-off, 10:47 p.m. outside apartment."

She stared at the blinking cursor, the weight of the day settling on her shoulders like a too-heavy blanket.

Somewhere back in the cottage, Emily's maze drawing was *probably* tucked into a folder marked *ART PORTFOLIO*. Somewhere in Willow Creek, a black SUV prowled the streets.

And Theresa Daye, who had always believed laughter was the best medicine, was starting to suspect that some stories didn't end with hugs.

Chapter Three

The next morning, Theresa arrived at Sunnybrook Cottage with the black SUV still burned into her retinas. She'd barely slept, replaying the engine's low growl and the way the headlights had pinned her like a spotlight. Strong black coffee, her third cup, sloshed in her travel mug as she fumbled with the keys.

Milo was already waiting on the porch, sitting cross-legged beside a plastic triceratops the size of a house cat.

"Doctor Dinosaur says you look like you swallowed a storm cloud," he announced.

Theresa managed a smile. "Storm clouds are just fluffy rain machines. Let's get you inside before the thunder starts."

Mia was in the kitchenette, wrestling with the ancient toaster that only worked if you sweet-talked it. She took one look at Theresa's face and set down the butter knife.

"Okay, spill. You've got the same expression you wore when Mrs. Hargrove tried to ban glitter."

Theresa hesitated, then pulled out her phone and showed Mia the second email, the one with Emily's full drawing. Mia's eyes widened.

"Holy crap, T. That's not okay."

"I know." Theresa's voice cracked. "And last night, there was this SUV on the street—"

"Slow down," Mia interrupted her. "Slow down and start from the creepy email and work your way to the stalker-mobile."

After the kids had all trickled in, they migrated to the backyard . The cottage's fenced play area was a postage stamp of green, bordered by lilac bushes and a tire swing that squeaked like a mouse with opinions. Theresa and Mia perched on the picnic table, keeping one eye on the sandbox where Priya was attempting to bury Milo up to his knees.

"Disgruntled parent?" Mia theorized, wiping sand off her jeans. "You *did* post about the poop volcano incident. Some people have no sense of humor about explosive poop."

Theresa shook her head. "This feels targeted. The sender knew Emily's name was on the drawing. I cropped it out."

Mia's sarcasm faltered. "You think someone's watching the cottage?"

The thought had kept Theresa awake. She glanced at the fence line, half expecting the black SUV to materialize between the slats.

"I don't know." Her tone was as flat as her mood. "I hope it's just a prank."

Mia shook her head. "You don't think it's a prank."

She repeated, "I don't know."

Inside, the morning unfolded in fits and starts. Circle time was derailed when Landon Hargrove insisted the letter *Q* stood for "quinoa-free." Snack time involved a heated debate over whether goldfish crackers counted as seafood. Theresa moved through it all on autopilot, her smile a mask that felt stretched far too tight.

Art corner was where the day cracked open.

Emily had claimed her usual table, but today she'd abandoned the black gel pen for a single red crayon. Theresa watched from the supply closet as Emily drew with fierce concentration, creating short, angry strokes that tore the paper in places. When Theresa approached, Emily didn't look up.

"Want to tell me about your picture, Em?"

Emily's crayon stilled. The page showed a cliff with jagged lines like broken teeth and a red stick figure tumbling headfirst toward a scribbled *X* at the bottom. A second figure stood at the cliff's edge, arms outstretched.

Theresa's stomach lurched. "Who's falling?"

Emily's whisper was barely audible. "The man who came to our house."

Before Theresa could press, there was a kerfuffle over at the block corner, and with the raised voices, the moment shattered. Emily folded the drawing in half, then in half again, and slipped it into Theresa's pocket.

The kids' lunchtime was a blur. Theresa texted Alex under the table. *Dinner tomorrow? Need to talk. Not about lavender lattes.*

His reply was instart. *Maple Café, 6:30. I'll bring the good cookies.*

Naptime arrived like a mercy. Theresa dimmed the lights and set the white noise machine to "ocean waves." Most kids conked out immediately, but Emily lay rigid, eyes fixed on the ceiling.

Theresa crouched beside her cot. "Sweet dreams, Em."

Emily's hand shot out, gripping Theresa's wrist with surprising strength. "Don't let the monsters find me."

Theresa's heart cracked. "No monsters here. Just Doctor Dinosaur and his stethoscope."

Emily's grip loosened, but her eyes stayed open until Theresa pretended to fall asleep in the rocking chair.

Pickup was controlled chaos between parents juggling briefcases and ballet bags and kids protesting the end of playtime. It was always a gratifying moment when the kiddos preferred daycare over going home, but it stressed out the parents.

Though not all parents, or rather guardians.

At pickup, Victor was late. Not for the first time.

Theresa watched Emily sit on the bench by the door, legs swinging, unicorn notebook open on her lap. Every time the bell chimed she looked up hopefully, then deflated when it wasn't her uncle.

At six twenty-two, almost half an hour past closing, he finally strode in, tie askew, phone to his ear. He held up one finger to Theresa, clearly signaling her to wait.

She didn't.

"Mr. Johnson, a word?"

He ended the call with a curt "I said I'll handle it" and turned the full force of his impatience on her.

"Emily's paperwork says six o'clock pickup. We close then."

"I was in a meeting."

"It happens. Next time I'll have to charge the late fee."

His eyes narrowed. "Is this about money?"

"No," Theresa said, voice steady. "It's about Emily waiting alone."

Something flickered across his face—anger, maybe guilt—but it was gone as quickly as it came.

"She's fine," he said, reaching for Emily's hand.

Emily took it, but her eyes found Theresa's across the room. A silent question.

Theresa answered with the smallest nod. *I see you.*

Victor didn't notice. He was already steering Emily out the door.

Mia locked the door. "You're telling me everything tonight. Wine mandatory."

Theresa promised, but her mind was already racing ahead to her apartment, to Google, to answers.

She arrived home, slipped off her shoes, and opened her laptop on the kitchen table. The search bar stared at her like a dare.

Victor Johnson Willow Creek

Results flooded in, including a professional profile (real estate developer, Johnson & Pike Properties) and a Chamber of Commerce photo from last year's gala, Victor shaking hands with the mayor.

Then, buried on page two, was the article she was looking for: "Leonard Pike, 44, Dies in Tragic Accident."

Theresa clicked. The obituary was sparse. "Beloved husband of Claire Pike, did not survive a fall on March 14. Ruled accidental by Wi low Creek PD."

Her pulse thrummed in her ears. She opened another tab, searched *Leonard Pike fall*. A local news article was the first result on the page.

"Police say Pike fell while discussing business at his partner's residence. No signs of foul play. Services are pending."

Was he on his own when he fell? Emily had drawn a second figure at the cliff's edge, after all.

Theresa's phone buzzed. She looked to see it was Alex confirming dinner one last time. She typed a quick *See you then* and kept digging. Property records showed Johnson & Pike owned half the commercial real estate in town, including the old mill by the river. There was a forum post from a disgruntled tenant: "Victor's all charm until you're late on rent. Then the goons show up."

Middle of the evening, her phone rang.

No Caller ID, so Theresa stared at the screen, thumb hovering. She answered on the fourth ring.

"Hello?"

Silence, then a male voice, distorted through what sounded like a bad voice changer.

"Names, Theresa. Or the cottage burns."

The line went dead.

Theresa's knees buckled. She sank to the floor, phone clutched to her chest. The apartment's silence pressed in, broken only by the hum of the refrigerator.

She called Mia.

"Hey, boss," Mia answered, laughter in the background. "Wine's chilling. You on your way?"

Theresa opened her mouth to tell her everything, spill all the information about the most recent threat, but the words stuck in her throat. If she involved Mia more than she already had, she was afraid she'd be painting a target on her back too.

"I'm absolutely fried," she lied, her voice steady despite the earthquake she was experiencing inside. "We had some day with the kiddos, huh? Can we do a rain check on wine?"

Mia's pause was heavy. "You sure? You sound—"

Theresa interrupted. "If I sound the way I feel, then I bet I sound exhausted. A lot of the kiddos were extra today. We can talk tomorrow. Love you, bye."

She hung up before Mia could argue.

Theresa opened her laptop again, created a new folder titled *EMILY – DO NOT DELETE*. Into the folder, she saved screenshots of both emails, the SUV photo, the obituary. Then she opened a private browser and searched *how to trace a blocked call*.

The results were useless. It was mostly about how to create an untraceable phone number and less about how to protect oneself from scammers. She skimmed the entries for spoofed numbers and burner apps, then bookmarked a site about surveillance cameras instead. It was the only thing of potential application she could find.

Not long before bedtime, she stood at her window again. Main Street was empty, but the hair on her neck prickled. She drew the curtains tight, double-checked the deadbolt, and wedged a chair under the doorknob for good measure.

In the bedroom, she pulled Emily's drawing from her purse, the one with the red stick figure. She unfolded it carefully. At the bottom, in Emily's careful block letters: *HE FELL.*

Theresa stared at the words until they blurred. Then she tucked the drawing into the folder, closed the laptop, and sat in the dark.

Outside, the wind picked up, rattling the fire escape. Somewhere in the distance, a dog barked once, then fell silent.

Theresa whispered to the empty room, "I'm not letting the monsters win."

But the promise tasted bitter on her tongue, like something she might not be able to come through with.

Chapter Four

Theresa woke to the sound of her own heartbeat. The chair was still wedged under the doorknob, the curtains drawn so tight not even a sliver of predawn slipped through. She checked her phone to find it was what her grandmother used to call the ass-crack of the morning. There were no missed calls and no new emails. The stifling silence felt like a held breath.

She showered in water hot enough to scald, then got dressed in the armor of her favorite cardigan, the soft teal one, slightly frayed threads at the cuffs a demonstration of it being her favorite. She drove to Sunnybrook Cottage before the sun had fully committed to rising above the rim of the horizon. The rainbow door looked garish in the dull gray light, almost like a promise someone had forgotten to keep.

Inside, she opened her laptop on the circle-time rug and refreshed *Kid Quips*. The *Maze Master* post had blown past 3,000 likes overnight. Tips totaled $62.47. And the comments—still, thank God, under the rule of moderation—were both humorous and a minefield.

She scrolled, stomach tightening with each new entry.

ParentOfThree: "My kid draws monsters too. Totally normal!"

CraftyMom22: "Love the mazes! Do you sell prints?"

AnonUser88: "Ask Maze Girl what Daddy did in the basement."

Theresa's finger froze over the delete button. The time stamp was 2:17 a.m. She approved the harmless ones, trashed the rest except for the weird one, then opened the blog's analytics. The *AnonUser88* comment had originated as a brand-new member of the blog from an IP in Willow Creek—same as the emails. Her hands shook as she copied the details into her *EMILY – DO NOT DELETE* folder.

Mia arrived at her normal time, took one look at Theresa's face, and poured coffee without asking questions. The kids trickled in. Emily was last, dropped off by Victor in their black sedan. He didn't even get out this time—just lowered the window and gestured imperiously, staying only long enough to sign the clipboard with that sharp slash of ink. Emily's braid was neater today, but her eyes were ringed with the purple of sleeplessness.

"Morning, Em," Theresa said, crouching to her level. "Want to help me set up the sensory table?"

Emily nodded, but her gaze darted to the art corner. The folded red-stick-figure drawing was back in Theresa's purse, burning a hole through leather and lining.

The day dragged. Circle time dissolved into a debate about whether clouds were made of cotton candy (Priya) or sheep farts (Milo). Snack time involved a spilled-juice incident that required three rolls of paper towels. Theresa moved through it all with mechanical smiles, her mind replaying the distorted voice: "Or the cottage burns."

Midmorning, she slipped into the supply closet and called the nonemergency police line. An officer picked up on the third ring, sounding like he'd swallowed gravel for breakfast.

"Willow Creek PD, Daniels."

Theresa gave him the condensed version of what was going on. She told him about the emails, the SUV, the phone threat, the basement comment. She emailed screenshots from her phone while she talked.

Daniels sighed so heavily she felt it through the receiver. "Look, Ms. Daye, kids draw weird stuff. My nephew once drew me as a potato with legs. And blog trolls? Change your passwords, enable two-factor. We get fifty of these a week."

"But the caller knew my name. And the cottage—"

"Pranksters escalate. Block the number, document everything. If something *physical* happens, like property damage, vandalism, or a break-in, be sure to call back.

Otherwise, you're tying up resources we need for real crimes."

Theresa bit back a retort about what constituted *real*. "Thank you for your time."

She hung up and stared at the supply closet shelves, filled with boxes of glitter glue, construction paper, and a jar of googly eyes that judged her silently. *Real crimes*. Like a man falling downstairs. Like an eight-year-old drawing cliffs in red crayon.

Lunch was sunbutter sandwiches again. Theresa ate half of hers standing up, watching Emily pick at crusts. The girl hadn't touched the art table all morning.

Thinking about the day ahead, Theresa texted Alex.

Maple Café still good? I might be running a little late.

His reply was instant.

Text me when you're available. I'll get us a table by the window. AND I will save you a decaf lavender latte.

She broke the seal with Mia, filling her in on everything that'd happened and that she'd learned so far. Then, leaving Mia with the kiddos, Theresa went to the police station. The waiting room smelled of burnt coffee and lemon disinfectant. Plastic chairs, a flickering fluorescent light, a poster about bicycle safety. She filled out a formal report, uncaring of Daniels's advice earlier in the day, and handed over prints of the emails and the SUV picture, as well as the call log. The desk sergeant took it with the enthusiasm of someone accepting a parking ticket.

"Daniels will review it," he said. "Might take a few days."

Theresa nodded, throat tight. *A few days. Plenty of time for a cottage to burn.*

Back at Sunnybrook, the afternoon had dissolved into barely tamed bedlam. Outdoor playtime was cut short by a sudden drizzle, which had kids shrieking as they raced inside, leaving muddy footprints like abstract art. Theresa mopped away the evidence while Mia wrangled damp sneakers into cubbies.

It took another whole effort from both of them to replace the kiddos' wet socks with daycare ones. Something about the bright yellow with grippy treads turned the kids off the change. Still, they worked at it until all feet were bright as sunshine and dry.

Victor arrived with less than five minutes to spare. He wore an obviously bespoke suit today. It was charcoal, and expensive, the kind that cost more than Theresa's monthly rent. His smile was dialed to eleven, all white teeth and practiced charm.

"Theresa, always a pleasure. And here I am, on time to pick up our sweet Emily." He signed the clipboard with a flourish. "She's been talking nonstop about your story time voices."

Theresa's stomach churned. "She's a joy. Very creative."

Victor's hand settled on Emily's shoulder as she approached, and Theresa watched as those fingers curled just a fraction too tight. Emily flinched, almost imperceptibly.

"Uncle Victor, can we go?" she asked in an uncommonly small voice.

"In a minute, princess." To Theresa he asked, "Any concerns I should know about? Behavioral? Social?"

The question hung between them like a blade. Theresa thought of the red crayon cliff, the basement comment, the distorted voice. She thought of Officer Daniels dismissing her with a potato analogy.

"Just settling in," she said. "New routines, especially after a profound loss will take time."

Victor's smile didn't waver, but his grip on Emily tightened more. "Of course. We're all adjusting."

He guided Emily toward the door. At the threshold, she glanced back with wide eyes, a silent plea Theresa couldn't decipher. Then they were gone, swallowed by the black sedan's tinted windows.

Mia locked the door behind them. "Okay, that man gives me serial-killer vibes. His suits are always just a little *too* perfect. Like he ironed his soul."

Theresa didn't laugh. She stood in the empty playroom, surrounded by abandoned toys and half-finished puzzles. The silence pressed in, heavy as wet wool.

Mia touched her arm "T, talk to me."

Theresa opened her mouth, closed it. Instead, she pulled the folded red drawing from her purse and smoothed it on the circle-time rug.

Mia's breath hitched. "Jesus. That's—"

"Grim, right? Emily drew it yesterday. Said it was 'the man who came to our house.'"

Mia stared at the cliff, the falling figure, the second stick person at the edge. "You think…?"

"I think Leonard Pike didn't fall on accident." Theresa's voice was steady now, iron forged in the fire of Daniels's dismissal and Victor's too-tight grip. "I think Emily saw something. And someone wants her quiet."

Mia's eyes flicked to the windows, the darkening street beyond. "What do we do?"

Theresa folded the drawing carefully and slipped it back into her purse. The cottage smelled of crayons and rain-damp sneakers, but beneath it lurked something sharper—fear, acrid and metallic.

"Today I went and filed an official report with the police. They'll only get involved if someone gets hurt or if there's damage to the property, so they won't do anything until it's too late. But you and me? We protect her," Theresa said. The words settled in her bones, solid as truth. *If no one else will, I will.*

She grabbed her keys. "Lock up tight. I'm meeting Alex. I'll text you when I'm home."

Outside, the drizzle had stopped, leaving the air thick and electric. Theresa scanned the street, but there was no black SUV, no idling shadows. Still, she walked to her car with her keys laced between her fingers like claws.

At the Maple Café, Alex was waiting with two lattes and a plate of finger sandwiches and a couple of oatmeal cookies. His smile faltered when he saw her face.

"Rough day?" he asked.

Theresa slid into the booth. "You have no idea."

She told him everything, from the comment meltdown, Daniels's dismissal, Victor's grip, and finally about the vow now burning in her chest. Alex listened without interrupting, his librarian calm cracking only when she described the phone threat.

"You need to stay somewhere else tonight," he said. "My sister's guest room—"

"I'm not running," Theresa cut him off as she wrapped her hands around the cooling mug. Lavender steam curled between them. "But what you said the other day, you're right. I could use a research partner. Someone who knows how to dig without leaving footprints."

Alex's eyes softened. "I've got microfiche access and a suspicious amount of free time."

Theresa managed a smile. It felt foreign, like trying on someone else's skin. "Monday? After pickup. I want to research security measures other daycares have in place."

They finished their lattes in companionable silence, the café's hum a buffer against the storm building inside her.

When Alex walked her to her car, he hesitated, hand on her arm. "Theresa." His voice was low. "Whatever this is, please know you're not alone."

She wanted to believe him. Wanted to lean into the solid warmth of his presence and let someone else carry even a portion of the weight. But Emily's drawing was in her purse, and Victor's fngerprints would be on Emily's shoulder, and the cottage—her safe place, her rainbow-door sanctuary—suddenly felt as fragile as construction paper.

"I know," she said. "But I'm the one who promised her no monsters."

Alex brushed a curl from her cheek. "Then we'll build a bigger night-light."

Back at her apartment, after texting Mia, Theresa opened her laptop one last time. The blog's dashboard glowed with the counter showing 3,412 likes. A new moderated comment waited.

AnonUser88: "Tick-tock, Miss T. Some cliffs have no bottom."

She printed it, deleted it, blocked the user, then opened a private browser and searched *how to install hidden cameras in a daycare*. The results were another rabbit hole, this one of nanny cams disguised as teddy bears and smoke detectors.

Theresa bookmarked three. Then she opened her *EMILY – DO NOT DELETE* folder and added a new note:

"Day 4 - Victor's grip. Police useless. Report filled out. Vow made. Next step will be eyes everywhere."

She closed the laptop, drew the curtains, and sat in the dark. Outside, Willow Creek slept under a thin veil of mist. Somewhere, a child drew cliffs in red crayon. Somewhere, a man in a perfect suit smiled too wide.

Theresa whispered into the silence, "Your move."

Chapter Five

The nap room at Sunnybrook Cottage was the one place in her life where for the space of an hour and a half, the world shrank to the size of twelve cots and the hush of sleeping children. Theresa had painted the ceiling pale blue and dotted it with glow-in-the-dark stars so that even the darkest dreams had somewhere to look. Today, the stars were glowing slightly, the room dimmed to a bruised twilight by blackout curtains. The white noise machine murmured ocean waves, a lullaby for the exhausted.

Theresa sat in the rocking chair she'd refinished herself, made out of soft pine, sanded smooth, with comfy cushions covered in a galaxy print. Her phone was on Airplane Mode, because while she guarded her charges, everything outside this orbit could wait. She watched the rise and fall of small chests, counted breaths like rosary beads.

Milo had kicked off his blanket again, still going a hundred miles an hour even in the depths of sleep, one sock dangling from a toe. Priya clutched a plush narwhal that was her frequent naptime companion. Emily lay perfectly still, eyes open, her stare fixed on the ceiling as if she could see through plaster and shingles to whatever waited beyond.

Theresa's own eyes were gritty. She'd slept maybe three hours, the rest spent scrolling nanny-cam reviews and staring at the red-stick-figure drawing until the lines blurred. In her mind's eye, Victor's grip on Emily's shoulder had left faint bruises, the child's skin marred by five pale fingerprints she couldn't unsee. Something she couldn't excuse.

A soft rustle. Emily had turned onto her side, facing Theresa. The girl's lips moved.

Theresa leaned forward, the chair creaking. "Em? You okay?"

Emily's whisper was barely air. "The man fell."

Theresa's heart stuttered. She slipped from the chair and knelt beside the cot, careful not to wake the others. "What man, sweetie?"

Emily's gaze flicked to the sleeping children, then back. "He came to our house. Yelled at Uncle Victor. Then he fell." A pause, so small it could break a heart, tears brimming in her eyes. "Uncle Victor said don't tell or the monsters come."

The words landed like stones in still water. Theresa kept her voice steady, the same tone she used for scraped knees and lost teeth. "Monsters hate the truth, Em. They're allergic. You told me the truth, so they're already sneezing."

Emily's mouth trembled, haltingly caught in a half smile, half sob. She reached under her pillow and pulled out a folded scrap of paper. Theresa recognized it as being from the unicorn notebook Emily carried everywhere. This page showed a drawing of the same red cliff, but now the falling figure had a face. There were two dots for eyes and a slash for a mouth open in a silent scream. The standing figure had no face at all.

Theresa refolded the drawing and put it into her pocket, next to the first one. "Thank you for trusting me. That was brave."

Emily's eyes fluttered closed, exhaustion winning at last. Theresa stayed kneeling until the girl's breathing evened out, then eased back to the rocking chair. Her pulse hammered so loudly she was sure it would wake the room.

When naptime ended, the children stirred like sleepy birds. Theresa helped with shoes and sweaters, her mind cataloging every detail of Emily's flinch when Milo hugged too hard, the way she kept one hand on her backpack strap as if anchoring herself to something solid.

Snack time was apple slices and string cheese, the kind of simple offering that usually sparked joy. But today the kids were subdued, seemingly picking up on the static in the air. Theresa hated that her mood might have touched the children, so she made a point to move among them, refilling water cups and wiping chins with a smile. Emily sat at the end table, backpack between her feet like a loyal dog.

Theresa crouched. "Want to help me pass out napkins for sticky fingers?"

Emily nodded. As she stood, the backpack tipped. A small gold glint rolled across the floor and stopped against Theresa's sneaker.

A cuff link. Tiny, heavy, engraved with swirling initials that made her breath catch in her chest: *L.P.*

Leonard Pike.

She palmed it before Emily noticed, slipping it into the same pocket as the drawings. The metal was cold, a secret weight against her thigh.

"Miss T, I dropped my cheese," Priya called.

Theresa forced a smile. "Coming."

The rest of snack time passed in a haze. Theresa's eyes kept drifting to Emily's backpack, to the empty space where the cuff link had been. How long had it been there? Had Victor seen it? The questions stacked like wooden blocks, one wrong move from collapse.

Mia took over cleanup so Theresa could "check inventory" in the supply closet. She locked the door, leaned against the shelves, and examined the cuff link under the flashlight of her phone. Solid 14-karat, the kind of thing that cost more than her monthly grocery budget. The back had a tiny scratch—someone had pried it from fabric in a hurry.

She photographed it from every angle, then sealed it in a sandwich bag labeled *EVIDENCE* in Sharpie. The word looked ridiculous among the glue sticks and pom-poms, but it steadied her.

The cottage was quiet again, as with fifteen minutes to spare, all the kids were gone, picked up by their harried caregivers. Mia was restocking the sensory bin with rainbow rice and Theresa was wiping down tables when the front door chimed. She froze. They were closed. The sign clearly said so.

Mia appeared in the hallway, eyebrows raised. "Delivery?"

Theresa shook her head and approached the door cautiously. No one on the porch. Just a plain white envelope slid halfway under the mat, her name typed in block letters.

She picked it up with two fingers, as if it might bite. Inside was a single sheet of printer paper, folded once.

"Cuff links are for grown-ups. Keep the kid quiet."

No signature. No return address. The paper was cheap, the kind sold in bulk at the office supply store over on Elm Street.

Theresa's knees went weak. She checked the lock on the door, leaned her forehead against the cool wood, and breathed through the panic.

Mia's voice floated from the playroom. "T? You okay?"

Theresa straightened, folded the note, and tucked it into her purse with the drawings and the bagged cuff link. "Fine. Just… junk mail."

Another lie. They were piling up like unread blog comments.

Mia didn't push. She knew Theresa well enough to sense when the dam was about to break.

Theresa spent the next half hour on autopilot while doing everyday necessary jobs of sweeping glitter and sanitizing toys, all while humming the cleanup song off-key. When Mia left, Theresa locked the cottage and stood in the empty playroom. The rainbow door felt suddenly childish, a target painted in primary colors.

She opened her laptop on the circle-time rug. The *Kid Quips* dashboard glowed, showing 3,800 likes on the *Maze Master* post. A new moderated comment waited.

AnonUser8888: "Gold still shines in the dark. Some treasures should stay buried."

Theresa documented, then deleted it, and finally disabled comments entirely. The blog had been her creative outlet, her side hustle, her joy. Now it felt like an anchor, dragging her down a little more every day.

She closed the laptop and looked around the room. The glow stars on the ceiling caught the last of the daylight, faint but stubborn. Emily's mazes still hung on the art wall, intricate and lonely.

Theresa's phone buzzed with a text from Alex.

Maple Café tomorrow? I couldn't wait till Monday, so I've got microfiche on Pike's business dealings. Also cookies.

She typed back. *I've got the festival to work. Meet me at Sunnybrook at 7 p.m. tomorrow? Bring flashlights.*

His response was almost instant. *I'm intrigued and only slightly terrified. Why don't you drop by the library Sunday when you're free so we can look at the microfiche stuff. Your convenience.*

"Good point," she whispered, then replied, *Okay.*

Okay, see you then.

Theresa pocketed the phone and stood in the middle of the playroom. The silence pressed in, thick with the ghosts of laughter and the weight of secrets.

She thought of Emily's whisper: *"Uncle Victor said don't tell or the monsters come."*

She thought of the cuff link, cold and silently accusing.

She thought of the note, slipped under the mat like a snake.

And she made a pivot. Sharp. Irreversible.

No more waiting for the police. No more hoping the threats were pranks. No more pretending the blog was just harmless fun.

Theresa Daye, daycare manager, blogger, collector of kid quips, had just become something else.

Protector. Sleuth. Guardian of a child who drew cliffs in red crayon and carried gold cuff links in her backpack.

She opened the supply closet and pulled out a toolbox she hadn't touched since installing the cubbies. Inside was a cordless drill, screws, and a tiny Allen wrench. She added the sandwich bag with the cuff link, the drawings, and the note.

Then she opened her phone and ordered three nanny cams—teddy bear, smoke detector, and a wall clock. Same-day shipping, should be at her apartment by ten.

Theresa locked the toolbox, set it by the rainbow door, and turned off the lights. The glow stars winked down at her, faint but fierce.

"Monsters," she whispered to the empty room, "you are about to learn what happens when you threaten my kids."

She took the toolbox, stepped outside, locked the door, and didn't look back. The pivot was complete. The game had changed.

And Theresa Daye was all in.

Chapter Six

The Willow Creek Kids Festival spilled across the town square like a patchwork quilt stitched from hay bales, fairy lights, and the smell of kettle corn. It was early Saturday morning, and the last blowout before school started was already humming with running kids in costumes, parents clutching sugar-laced everything, and even a brass band warming up near the gazebo.

Theresa had volunteered Sunnybrook Cottage for a booth months ago, back when her biggest worry was whether the glitter glue would arrive in time. Now the booth felt like a stage, and she was the unwilling star.

She and Mia had set up at dawn, with a six-foot table draped in primary colors and a banner reading *KID QUIPS 2025 CALENDARS – $15 EACH*. The calendars were her pride and joy—a full twelve months of anonymized kid quotes, each paired with a watercolor illustration by a local art student. January had "Clouds are sky sheep who forgot how to land." February was "Love is when your goldfish shares its bubbles." She'd paid to print five hundred, then stored them in the cottage's supply closet like contraband.

Mia handed her a coffee the size of a small bucket. "You look like you're about to sell state secrets, not calendars."

"Feels that way," Theresa muttered. She'd barely slept.

Alex had texted before dawn. *Claire Pike lives at 28 Maple Lane. Works Saturdays at the library book sale table. I'll be at the festival tomorrow, or I guess later today. I'll be the dashing mystery assistant in a baby blue hoodie, posted near the Ferris wheel.*

Theresa wore a denim jacket over a Sunnybrook T-shirt, hair in a braid to keep it out of her face when she inevitably knelt to tie someone's shoe. She plastered on her daycare smile, which had the façade of being warm and forever unflappable, and began rearranging calendars in somehow neater stacks.

The first hour was a blur of familiar faces. Mrs. Hargrove bought three calendars, sniffed at the lack of quinoa-friendly recipes, and left a pamphlet on screen-time reduction on the table. Theresa filed it away in an empty box under the table, along with crumpled pieces of packing tape. Priya's mom teared up at the goldfish bubbles quote. Nathan's dad tried to pay with a fistful of arcade tokens.

Midmorning, Mr. Delgado, the baker from Sweet Rise with a mustache like a push broom, stopped by with a tray of cherry whoopie pies. He set one on the table like a bribe.

"On the house, Miss T. You do such a great job with the kiddos. I sure love those kidisms."

Theresa accepted the treat. "Thank you so much. Tell me, Mr. D—any gossip worth a whoopie pie?"

He leaned in, voice dropping. "Victor Johnson bought the old mill last month. Cash deal. Word is he's got investors from out of state. Some of those shady types. My cousin's on the zoning board, and she says the permits are a mess."

Theresa's pulse quickened. "Shady how?"

"Shell companies. One's registered to a PO box in the Caymans." Delgado winked. "But you didn't hear it from me."

He moved on, tray two whoopies lighter.

Theresa jotted "mill – Caymans" in her phone notes, then looked up to see Claire Pike approaching.

Leonard's widow was thinner than in the gala photo, cheekbones sharp under red-rimmed eyes. She wore a library volunteer badge and carried a canvas tote stuffed with paperbacks. Her gaze flicked over the calendars, lingered on the booth banner.

"Are these the famous Kid Quips?" Her voice was hoarse, like she'd been crying or smoking, or both.

Theresa nodded. "Fifteen dollars supports new playground equipment."

Claire pulled out a crumpled twenty, eyes on the January page. "My husband used to say kids see through adults like glass. Guess he was right."

Theresa's throat tightened. "I'm sorry for your loss."

Claire's laugh was brittle. "Accidental fall, they said. Leonard didn't drink. Didn't stumble. He was *pushed*." The last word cracked like ice.

Theresa glanced around; thankfully there was no one close enough to hear. "Do you know why?"

Claire's fingers tightened on the twenty. "Money. Always money. Victor wanted him gone. Wanted us out of the partnership. Didn't like the way we insisted on aboveboard practices." She shoved the bill across the table, took a calendar, and walked away before Theresa could give her change, or more importantly, ask more questions.

Mia appeared at her elbow. "That was Leonard Pike's wife, right? She looked like she'd seen a ghost."

"Or made one," Theresa murmured.

The festival swelled. A clown on stilts wove through the crowd. The brass band launched into "Sweet Caroline," and half the square sang along. Theresa sold calendars on autopilot, her mind spinning. *Pushed. Mill. Caymans.*

Finally, just before lunch, Victor Johnson arrived.

He wore a stylish camel coat despite the mild weather, Emily trailing behind in a purple dress with a cape, the unicorn notebook clutched to her chest. Victor's smile was festival-bright, but his eyes scanned the crowd like a hawk.

"Theresa!" he called. waving. "Emily insisted on the bouncy castle."

Emily's gaze darted to the booth, then away.

Theresa crouched in front of her. "Hey, witchling. Save me a spell?"

Emily managed a nod, but her knuckles were white on the notebook.

Victor steered her toward the inflatable castle, which was a blue dragon with a slide for a tongue. Theresa watched them go, then texted Alex.

Victor here with Em. Bouncy castle. Eyes open.

Alex responded, *Copy. Ferris wheel in 5.*

Theresa handed the booth over to Mia. "Can you cover me? Bathroom run."

Mia's eyebrow arched, but she nodded.

Theresa wove through the crowd, keeping Victor in sight. He lifted Emily into the bouncy castle, then stepped back to take a call. Emily bounced once, twice, then froze. Her eyes locked on something beyond the dragon's tail.

Theresa followed her gaze. A man in a black cap and sunglasses stood near the cotton candy stand, arms crossed. Tall, broad-shouldered, a scar visible on his jaw when he turned. This was Victor's associate—Theresa had seen him in a Chamber of Commerce photo, captioned "Raymond 'Ray' Moreau, Johnson & Pike Security Consultant."

Emily's face crumpled. She dropped to her knees in the bouncy castle, crawling toward the exit slide.

Theresa moved without thinking, pushing through clusters of families.

"Em!" she called.

Emily tumbled down the slide, landed hard, and bolted, not toward Victor but straight into the crowd. Theresa lost her for a heartbeat, then spotted the purple cape disappearing behind the funnel cake trailer.

She gave chase, dodging strollers and corn dog sticks. Emily ducked into the bouncy-castle line again, burrowed under a pile of discarded shoes, and curled into a ball.

Theresa knelt, heart hammering. "It's okay, sweetie. It's me."

Emily's voice was muffled. "Uncle Ray. He's mad at Uncle Victor."

Theresa's blood ran cold. She peeled back a sneaker to reveal Emily's tear-streaked face. "You're safe. I promise."

She helped Emily out, keeping the girl's hand in hers. Victor was still on his phone, back turned. Ray had vanished.

Theresa led Emily to the booth. Mia took one look at her and grabbed a juice box. "Sit, witchling. Sugar, stat."

Emily sipped, trembling. Theresa crouched in front of her. "Want to tell me about Uncle Ray?"

Emily shook her head, but her eyes flicked to the Ferris wheel. Theresa followed her gaze—Victor and Ray now stood behind the ride's control booth, heads bent in heated conversation. Victor's hand slashed the air while Ray's jaw visibly clenched.

Theresa pulled out her phone, zoomed in, and snapped several photos. The men were partially obscured by the wheel's shadow, but the tension was clear.

Victor glanced up, spotted Theresa. His expression shifted when she waved at him, first in surprise, then something colder. He ended the conversation and strode over. If feet could be angry, they'd stomp the way his feet were stomping.

"Emily, time to go." His tone left no room for argument.

Emily clung to Theresa's leg. "I wanna stay."

Victor's smile was glass. "We have plans, princess."

Theresa met his eyes. "She's upset. Maybe give her a minute?"

Victor's hand settled on Emily's shoulder with the same brutal grip as before. "Family matter."

He guided Emily away. She looked back once, eyes pleading. Theresa memorized the set of Victor's shoulders, the way Ray fell into step behind them like a bodyguard.

Mia exhaled. "That man's charm is a weapon."

Theresa uploaded the photos to her secure cloud, then opened the festival map on her phone. The old mill was marked on the edge of town—abandoned, boarded up. *Shady investors*.

She texted Alex, *Photos uploaded. Change of plans. Need to go to the mill tonight. Pick me up at my house? 10 p.m.*

Alex texted back: *I'll be the one bringing bolt cutters.*

Theresa was laughing so hard she nearly had to make that bathroom run she'd lied about.

The festival continued, but Theresa moved through it like a ghost. She sold the last calendar, pocketed $7,505 in cash for the playground fund, and packed up with Mia, ready to head home.

"You're scaring me," Mia said as they loaded boxes into Theresa's car. "Whatever this is, you don't have to do it alone."

Theresa hugged her. "I know. But some doors I have to open myself."

Mia's eyes searched hers. "Wine soon. No excuses."

"Promise."

Theresa drove home, showered off festival sweat, changed into dark jeans and a black hoodie, and waited for night.

At the agreed-upon time, Alex pulled up outside her apartment. After she climbed into the truck, he handed her a thermos of cocoa and a flashlight.

"The mill itself is fenced," he said, "but there's a service gate on the east side. I scoped it this afternoon. Little tiny chain holding it closed."

"So you were serious about the bolt cutters?" Theresa grinned. "Good to know you're always prepared."

"I try." His somber tone killed her threatening giggles.

"Thank you, Alex. I don't know what I would have done if I didn't have your help in all of this. Probably have gone a little crazy."

"You mean crazier. You're already a little crazy. I'm the crazy-proof friend "

"I cannot dispute the truth of that statement." She lifted her mug of cocoa and gave it a sip. The sweet chocolatey goodness helped calm the rest of her nerves.

They drove the rest of the way in silence. In the truck's mirrors, the town lights faded behind them. The mill loomed on the riverbank, a study in darkness. The building was three stories of brick and broken windows, a relic of Willow Creek's logging days. A chain-link fence surrounded it, topped with razor wire. A Johnson & Pike sign read *FUTURE SITE OF RIVERBEND LOFTS – COMING 2026*.

Alex cut the chain with bolt cutters from his trunk. They slipped through, flashlights off, guided only by moonlight.

Inside, the mill was a cavern of shadows. Dust motes danced in the moonbeams. Old machinery crouched along the walls looking like sleeping beasts. A steady *crunch-crunch* came from underfoot as their shoes ground broken glass into a thousand pieces.

They found the office on the second floor. The door was standing ajar, a new lock recently installed yet simply not engaged.

The room was a construction zone. There were blueprints on the walls, a laptop on a folding table, and a series of file boxes labeled *INVESTORS*. Theresa opened one. Inside were contracts, offshore account numbers, and a ledger showing transfers of $500,000 chunks to a company called Cayman Tide Holdings.

Alex whistled. "Victor's laundering through the mill."

Theresa's flashlight caught a photo pinned to a corkboard. It was of Victor, Ray, and a third man she didn't recognize, standing in front of the mill. On the back, written in Sharpie, was "Phase 1 complete. L.P. out."

Her blood ran cold.

L.P. out.

Leonard Pike.

A noise downstairs of metal on concrete, followed by heavy footsteps.

Alex killed his flashlight. Theresa's heart slammed against her ribs as she did the same.

They ducked behind a stack of boxes. The footsteps climbed the stairs, slow and deliberate. A flashlight beam swept the room, catching dust and cobwebs.

A low male voice said, "Boss said check the office. Make sure nothing's disturbed."

Another voice, Victor's, closer than Theresa expected. "We should be coasting by now, Ray. Instead, we're working way too hard."

If he's not the "boss," then who is? That third man in the photo?

Victor continued, "Kids Festival was a mistake. That woman's asking questions."

Theresa's hand found Alex's in the dark. He squeezed once.

The flashlight beam passed inches from their hiding spot. Theresa held her breath.

"Find the planner," Victor ordered. "If she finds it, we're done."

The beam lingered on the file boxes, then moved on.

"There's nothing here, Victor. I need to go check on our chick, make sure she's staying in her roost like she should be."

"Yeah, nothing here."

Footsteps retreated back down the stairs, and a door screeched across the floor before it was slammed, followed by silence.

Theresa exhaled shakily and whispered, "They know."

Alex's voice was grim. "We need to get out. Now."

"How long before we can leave? We didn't even hear a vehicle."

"I say we wait five minutes."

"Five minutes." Theresa nodded. "Okay. I can do anything that long."

They waited the prescribed five minutes, then slipped downstairs and out the service gate. Alex fiddled with the chain until it looked locked again.

They had escaped, leaving no trace.

In the truck, Theresa opened an empty sandwich bag and stored a single page torn from the ledger, showing a $2.3 million transfer. *What on earth could that be about?*

They drove back under a sky full of stars, the mill's shadow shrinking in the rearview. The festival's joy felt a lifetime away.

But Emily's meltdown in the bouncy castle, Claire's cracked whisper, the ledger's cold numbers—they were real.

And tomorrow, Theresa would make them count.

Chapter Seven

On Sunday, Theresa arrived at the empty Sunnybrook Cottage before the sun had fully cleared the rooftops, the sky a watercolor wash of lilac and honey. The rainbow door looked almost solemn in the half-light, as if it knew what the day held. She unlocked it with steady fingers, no trembling today. The pivot had hardened something inside her.

Inside, she moved with purpose. First, she deployed the nanny cams. The teddy bear went on the bookshelf, the fake smoke detector was positioned high on the wall above the circle-time rug, and the last selection, a wall clock that did in fact work to tell analog time—a skill set that everyone could use—was angled toward the art corner.

"I'm sorry," she whispered to the empty room. "Sometimes love looks like spying."

She synced them to the app on her phone and tested the feeds. Crisp, silent, always watching.

Mia texted early. *You're at the daycare on Sunday? I saw your car, T. You hate when we have to work on Sundays. What's going on?*

Theresa replied, *Catching up on some work. I'll see you tomorrow.*

Mia wouldn't leave it alone. *Only if you promise wine and full disclosure later.*

Theresa sent back a quick *Sauvignon deal.*

She locked the cottage and drove to the Willow Creek Public Library, the cuff link in its sandwich bag riding shotgun like a tiny gold conscience. She'd left the rest of the evidence in the toolbox at her apartment.

Alex was behind the counter, and as he walked to unlock the front door, he eyed the two paper cups of coffee she brought in. He ushered her into the hushed space, and she took in a deep breath. The library smelled of old paper and lemon polish, the same welcoming scents as always, but today it felt like a vault. Echoed by the click of the lock behind them.

"This is me waiving the 'no food and drink' rule because you are a goddess who brought me the elixir of life."

"Decaf for you," she said, handing one over. "Figured you'd be wired enough."

Alex took it with a glare. "I don't get wired. Just a little jittery. Anyway, ready for basement archives?"

"Lead on."

"Follow me."

He took them past the children's section where a cardboard castle still stood from last week's story hour, then through a locked door and down a narrow staircase that creaked under their weight. The basement itself was a labyrinth of metal shelves, filled with boxes labeled in fading Sharpie.

WILLOW CREEK GAZETTE 1987–1992, CHAMBER OF COMMERCE MINUTES, OBITUARIES 2000–PRESENT

Alex pointed at a folder on the top step of a step stool. "Pike's file should be here. I pulled it already."

The manila folder was thin but heavy with possibility. Theresa opened it on a dusty table beneath a single hanging bulb.

"LEONARD J. PIKE

Born March 12, 1979 – Died March 14, 2024

Age 44

Net worth at time of death was listed at $2.3 million per the probate filing.

Survived by wife, Claire Pike; no children."

$2.3 million. The same amount as the transfer in the ledger.

A grainy photo from a charity gala featured Leonard in a tux, his arm around a beautiful blonde woman in emerald silk. Claire's smile looked practiced, the kind that hurt to hold.

Theresa flipped to the obituary from the *Willow Creek Gazette*. Same sparse details, that it was an accidental fall, no foul play, ending with private services, family asking for privacy in their grief. But a smaller clipping from the police blotter caught her eye.

"March 14 – 911 call from 1427 Riverbend Lane at 11:12 p.m. Caller (male) reported 'man fell downstairs.' Victim pronounced on scene. No signs of forced entry."

1427 Riverbend Lane. She knew that address—it was Victor's sleek modernist house on the hill, all glass and steel. But before it had been his, the Pikes had lived there.

Alex whistled low. "Accidental fall, my ass."

Theresa's phone buzzed. A nanny-cam alert because it had caught motion in the playroom. She opened the app to find nothing more than a dust mote drifting through a sunbeam. False alarm. Still, her pulse spiked.

"Microfiche?" she asked.

Alex led her to a corner machine, its screen flickering like an old TV. He loaded a reel labeled *GAZETTE – MARCH 2024*. They scrolled through grainy pages until they found it: "Local Businessman Dies in Freak Accident."

"Johnson & Pike Properties co-founder Leonard Pike, 44, was pronounced dead Thursday night after a fall in his partner's home. Victor Johnson, who discovered the body, told police the two were reviewing quarterly figures when Pike excused himself to use the restroom.

Johnson heard a crash and found Pike at the bottom of the basement stairs. Alcohol is not believed to be a factor. The case is closed pending autopsy."

Theresa's stomach turned. Basement stairs. Emily's whisper: *"Uncle Victor said don't tell or the monsters come."*

She photographed every page, her hands steady now. The librarian in Alex watched her with something like awe.

"You're terrifying when you're focused," he said.

"Scared people are dangerous," she replied. "I'm way past scared and into the realm of terrified."

They spent another hour digging, looking up property records that backed up what Theresa had found on her own. Records showed how Johnson & Pike owned half the commercial real estate in town. Something she hadn't known was a settled lawsuit from a tenant alleging strong-arm tactics. Finally, there was a Chamber of Commerce photo of Victor and Leonard shaking hands over a model of the old mill. In every picture, Victor's smile was too wide, and Leonard's eyes very tired.

Theresa's phone buzzed again, this time a text from an unknown number.

Curiosity killed the cat. Some doors stay closed for a reason.

She showed Alex. His jaw tightened.

"We're being watched?" He shook his head. "How would they know anything?"

Theresa looked around the basement, long shadows pooling in each corner, the hum of the microfiche machine the only sound. "I don't know, but let's give them something to watch."

She opened her blog on her phone and drafted a post titled *BLOG HIATUS*.

"Hey Quipsters,

Life's throwing some curveballs, and the kiddos need my full attention. Taking a break to focus on the playroom. Back when the glitter settles. Love you all.

—Miss T"

She hit Publish, then disabled comments entirely. The dashboard showed 4,012 likes on the *Maze Master* post. Tips had climbed to $89.47. She transferred the money to her savings—an emergency fund, she told herself. For legal fees, maybe. Or bail.

Alex watched her. "You sure about this?"

"Someone's using my blog to threaten a child. It stops now."

They left the library at noon, the sun high and merciless. Theresa's car felt too small, the cuff link burning a hole in her purse. She drove to the cottage, changed into jeans and a hoodie, and waited.

Early afternoon, her phone chimed with a call from Victor Johnson. It came into her second line, the number from the contact form on the website. *Interesting.*

"Theresa, hi. I didn't realize you were closed on Sundays. Emily left her unicorn notebook at the daycare. Any chance I could swing by to pick it up?"

Her blood ran cold. *Him, in her space. Now.*

"Of course," she said, voice bright. "I'm here. I should be done with my work midafternoon, so if you could come around 3 p.m., that would work best for me."

"I'll see you then." The call disconnected immediately, nearly before she could pull the phone from her ear.

She texted Alex. *Victor Johnson just called. Wants to stop by at 3. I'd love to have you on standby.*

His reply came quickly. *I'll be outside before 3. Say the word.*

Victor arrived a couple of minutes early, his black sedan gleaming like a shark. He wore a navy blazer over a white shirt, no tie. The look must be like casual Friday for millionaires. Emily wasn't with him.

"Theresa," he said, smile once again dialed to eleven. "Thanks for letting me come by."

She led him through the playroom, pointing out the sensory table, the reading nook, the art wall where Emily's mazes still hung. Victor's eyes lingered on them.

"Impressive operation," he said. "Emily speaks highly of you."

"She's a bright kid." Theresa's pulse hammered. "Unicorn notebook's in the office. Let me grab it."

The office was a converted closet, holding only a tiny desk, a short filing cabinet, and a window overlooking the backyard. Victor followed her in, filling the small space with expensive cologne and quiet menace.

Theresa opened the drawer where she'd stashed a decoy notebook. It was pink, sparkly, and definitely not Emily's, but had been a project with the plans of trading Emily for hers. Now she was glad she had it at hand. She noticed the drawer underneath was partially open, not how she'd normally leave it. *Was it like that earlier? I need to pay closer attention to the details now.* As she turned, Victor was a ready leaning toward the desk, fingers brushing the stack of parent files.

"Looking for something?" she asked.

He straightened, smile unwavering. "Just admiring the organization. You run a tight ship."

Theresa handed him the notebook. "Here you go."

Victor took it, but his eyes flicked to the filing cabinet. "Mind if I use your restroom? Long drive."

"Of course. Down the hall, second door."

The second he left, Theresa moved. The partially pulled drawer was a glaring sign that someone had messed with it.

She opened the drawer, heart in her throat. Inside was a leather-bound day-planner, monogrammed *LJP*. Leonard's.

How did it end up here?

Emily must've brought it in Friday.

But when would she have had time to put it in the drawer?

Theresa flipped it open with trembling fingers. Pages of meetings, scribbled numbers, a coffee stain on February 28. The last entry was on March 14.

"V.J. 9 p.m. – final numbers. Bring proof."

Proof. Of what?

Footsteps in the hall. Theresa shoved the planner into her hoodie pocket, closed the drawer, and stepped back just as Victor reappeared.

"All good?" he asked.

She nodded, leading him out. Her phone buzzed in her pocket, a text from Alex.

Sedan still here. You okay?

She kept one eye on Victor as they walked through the daycare. *Yeah, all good. He's leaving now.*

Victor paused again at the art wall to admire the mazes. "Emily's work?"

"Yes."

He touched one page held to the wall with sticky tack, tracing the path with a finger. "She's always been observant."

Theresa's skin crawled with goose bumps. "Kids see everything."

Victor's smile thinned, lips flattening. "Some things are better remaining unseen."

He left with the replacement notebook in hand. Theresa locked the door behind him, then sagged against it, planner clutched to her chest.

Alex burst in through the back, eyes wild. "What the hell was that?"

"Proof," Theresa said, holding up the planner. "This was in my desk just now. I don't remember looking at that drawer Friday, so Emily could have brought it in and slipped it into what she would think of as safekeeping. Leonard Pike was meeting Victor Johnson that night. About 'final numbers.' And Victor just tried to case my office."

Alex took the planner, flipping to the last page. "Jesus. This is evidence."

"Which is why we're not giving it to Daniels yet." Theresa's voice was steel. "He'll bury it. We need more."

Alex looked at her—really looked. "You're not the same woman who blogged about goldfish croutons."

"No," she said. "I'm the woman who's going to keep Emily alive."

They spent the next hour in the nap room, lights dim, planner spread on the galaxy-print rug. Alex photographed every page. Theresa cross-referenced dates with the microfiche articles. Victor had been liquidating assets, selling shares in Johnson & Pike to an offshore account.

The night Leonard died, he was bringing proof of embezzlement to confront Victor, his partner.

That meant Victor had motive.

Theresa opened her laptop one last time. The hiatus post had 1,200 likes. She drafted an email to her subscribers.

Subject line: *Thank You & Goodbye (For Now)*

"Quipsters,

The playroom is my heart. Right now, it needs all of me. Thank you for the laughs, the tips, the love. I'll be back Quipping when it's safe to share stories again.

—Miss T"

She hit Send, then disabled the blog's social media accounts. The immediate silence was deafening.

Alex watched her. "You're burning it all down."

"Controlled burn only," she corrected. "To save what matters."

They left the cottage at dusk, planner locked in Theresa's glove compartment. Alex followed her home in his truck, a silent escort. At her apartment, he carried in a pizza, loaded with pepperoni, extra cheese, and the kind of comfort that tasted like childhood.

They ate on the floor, backs against the couch and the planner open between them.

"What now?" Alex asked.

Theresa stared at the cuff link, the drawings, the note, having laid everything out for him to see. "Now we talk to Claire Pike. If anyone knows what 'final numbers' means, it's the widow."

Alex nodded. "Is tomorrow soon enough?"

"Plenty soon. We'll figure out the right time to get in touch with her."

He left much later, promising to text when he was home. Theresa locked the door, wedged the chair under the knob, and sat at her window. Main Street was quiet, but she watched anyway.

At 11:12 p.m., which was the exact time of the 911 call about Leonard's fall, a black SUV cruised past, slow as a shark. It didn't stop.

Theresa didn't flinch.

She opened the planner to March 14 one last time.

"V.J. 9 p.m. – final numbers. Bring proof."

Proof was in her hands now.

And tomorrow, she'd start digging graves with it.

Chapter Eight

On Monday, a woman in a navy blazer arrived during outdoor play.

"Sarah Mendoza, Department of Family Services."

Theresa's stomach dropped.

"Hello. Do you have some identification?"

"Of course." Sarah pulled out an ID sleeve from her crossover purse.

Theresa reviewed the very official credentials of a child protective services case manager. "You're legit."

Sarah's smile was kind but professional. "Routine follow-up. We received a concern about one of your children. May I observe?"

"Of course." Theresa wanted to ask who reported it. *I wonder if it was Daniel's, covering his ass with a just-in-case move.* Instead, she led Sarah to the backyard and prayed Emily wouldn't draw another cliff today.

Emily didn't draw at all. She spent the entire outdoor time glued to Theresa's side, silent, watching Sarah Mendoza with storm-cloud eyes.

When Sarah left, she handed Theresa a card. "If anything changes—anything at all—call me directly."

Theresa tucked the card into her bra like contraband.

Chapter Nine

Alex grinned at her over the counter at the library. "To what do I owe the pleasure of your presence?"

"I have an idea I wanted to run past you." She shrugged. "Plus, I wanted to see you. Can't a girl take a break once in a while?"

"If you were anyone other than Theresa Daye, and had a job you hated instead of loved, then I'd say a pop-up visit wouldn't earn even a raised eyebrow. But you are, and you love the kids, so...what kind of trouble are we about to get into?"

It had been a quiet few days. Unremarkable days of the daycare's standard drop-off drama and pickup blues. Even Emily had been playing more with Milo and the other kids. Theresa and Mia had been waiting for the other shoe to drop, but it seemed they were completely on the other side of things.

It had given Theresa time to look up more info online, but it was hard to make sense of it. She needed someone to bounce ideas around with.

She smiled. "We're just going to do a little bit of internet sleuthing, if you're up for the hunt."

"Oh, Theresa, I'd be up for a hunt anytime you need a wingman. Have you found out more about Leonard and Victor?"

"Maybe. Can I interest you in a take-out pizza for dinner tonight? My place?"

Alex's mouth spread in a slow grin, and then he blushed, the rose color rising up his throat until the tips of his ears burned bright red. He choked, coughed, and said, "It'd be my pleasure."

"Good. Daycare closes at six o'clock, so I'll run by after to pick up a pizza. Do you have a preference?"

"Nope, whatever you get will be fine." He looked her in the eyes. "I'll be there with bells on. It'd take a natural disaster to keep me away."

"Okay." Theresa felt her own face begin to flush, and she mentally rolled her eyes. "I better get going. The boss at the daycare is pretty strict on breaks."

"Theresa?"

She turned back to the counter, finding Alex had made his way around the end and was now within a couple of feet. "Yeah?"

"I can't wait."

The flush felt hotter, and Theresa kept her gaze locked with his. "Me either."

Chapter Ten

Theresa's apartment smelled of burnt toast and sleeplessness. She'd been up since the early hours, the mill's ledger page spread on her kitchen table like a crime-scene photo. The $2.3 million transfer stared back at her, Leonard Pike's net worth funneled into Cayman Tide Holdings the day after his death. Victor's signature was on every line.

Alex had crashed on her couch, still in yesterday's clothes, and rested on his back with one arm flung over his eyes. His position was somehow reminiscent of Milo, and she smiled fondly, her heart beating double time for a minute or so.

His laptop glowed on the coffee table, a window open to a dark-web forum where someone was selling "untraceable Cayman accounts—DM for details." Theresa had bookmarked it, then closed the tab before she did something stupid like reply.

A couple of hours later, her phone buzzed with an email alert from the *Kid Quips* backup server. She'd shut the blog down, but the domain still existed, like a ghost in the machine.

The email said "New Post Published – Title: *Who got lost?*"

Theresa's stomach dropped. She opened the link on her phone.

The blog was live again. Front and center was Emily's *exact* maze drawing, the one Theresa had cropped for anonymity. This version was of just the maze, but it was uncropped, Emily's name scrawled in purple marker in the bottom corner, her face softly out of focus. Beneath it, a caption in bold:

"Who got lost?"

No byline. No date. Just the drawing and a comment section already flooding with fire emojis and skull GIFs.

Theresa's hands shook so badly she nearly dropped the phone. She woke Alex with a shake.

"Someone hacked the blog. They posted Emily's full drawing."

Alex sat up, hair sticking out like a hedgehog. "Show me."

He took the phone, fingers flying. "Backend access. They used an old admin login—probably brute-forced it." He moved to his laptop and used Theresa's account to connect to the blog's server. Lines of code scrolled.

"Give me half a minute to change the admin access to two-factor and I'll look up the IP address," he muttered. A moment later he said, "Got it. Willow Creek Coffee Roasters. Time stamp 3:47 a.m."

Theresa's mind raced The coffee shop on Elm Street had free Wi-Fi, was open 24/7, and had security cameras that probably hadn't worked since the flood of '22.

"We need to see who was there," she said.

Alex was already pulling on his shoes. "We can catch my buddy at the shop. He owes me for fixing his POS system."

They made their way out the door, the sky still bruised with night. Willow Creek Coffee Roasters was a converted gas station, neon *OPEN* sign flickering. Inside, the barista, Darius, with a gorgeous septum piercing and sporting a sleeve of tattoos, was wiping down the espresso machine.

"Alex! Thought you were off caffeine." Darius grinned, then saw Theresa's face. "Uh-oh. Miss T?"

Alex slid a twenty across the counter. "I need to see your security footage from 3:30 to 4:00 a.m. Please."

Darius pocketed the bill. "It's in the back room, same setup you should remember. But if the health inspector asks, you were never here."

The footage was grainy, time-stamped. At 3:42 a.m., an imposing figure in a black hoodie entered, hood up, face obscured. They sat at the corner table, the one Theresa knew had the strongest Wi-Fi signal, opened a laptop, typed for seven minutes, then left.

"I can't believe they actually have security cameras." She leaned closer, throat tensing. "Can you zoom?"

Alex enhanced the frame. The hoodie had a logo on the sleeve. A very familiar one.

Sunnybrook Cottage Daycare – Staff

Theresa's blood ran cold. Only three people had those hoodies: her, Mia, and the part-time aide who'd quit in August.

Alex met her eyes. "Mia?"

Theresa was already dialing. Mia picked up on the second ring, voice thick with sleep.

"T? It's barely seven."

"Where were you at 3:45 a.m.?"

A pause. "Home. Why?"

"Coffee Roasters. Someone in a Sunnybrook hoodie hacked my blog. Posted Emily's drawing."

Mia's sharp inhale crackled through the phone. "I need to tell you something. Meet me at the cottage. Soon as you can." She paused, then half sobbed, "I'm so sorry."

Theresa and Alex were there in ten minutes. Mia opened the rainbow door, still in pajamas, hair a wild halo. She led them to the nap room, opened her laptop on the galaxy rug near a quietly sleeping Milo.

"I didn't want to tell you," she said, voice trembling. "Didn't want you to think I betrayed you."

She opened a browser tab that was set to show her bank account. Balance: -$4,312.87. Then an email chain with Victor Johnson.

Subject line: *Payment Plan – Torres, M.*

"Mia,

Your brother's debt is $12,000. Pay $1,000 monthly or collection begins. First payment due 6/15.

—V.J."

Theresa's knees weakened. "Your brother?"

Mia's eyes were glassy. "Javier. He's been in Vegas. Gambling. Victor holds his marker. I've been paying what I can, but it's never enough." She clicked another tab, this one the standard security footage from the cottage, time-stamped 3:20 a.m. that morning.

The camera showed a male figure in the Sunnybrook hoodie entering with a key. He went to the art wall and retrieved a piece of paper, then left.

Theresa's world tilted. "That's who posted Emily's drawing?"

Mia burst into tears. "I think it was my brother. He showed up a couple of days ago, says he's got a way to pay off his marker. Victor made me let him stay. Said if I didn't, he'd send Ray to collect from Javi immediately, and very much in person. You know what that kind of threat means. I don't know for sure it's Javi, but my hoodie is missing. He wasn't home when you called, and I didn't take long, but I looked through the room he's staying in. No hoodie in there either."

Alex's voice was gentle. "Mia, you should've told us."

"I know." She wiped her face with her sleeve. "I still have access from your vacation last year, so I logged in and deleted the post as soon as I saw it live. But the damage was already done."

Theresa opened the blog on Mia's laptop to find the post was gone, but the internet never forgot. Screenshots were already circulating on local social media groups.

Theresa's doubt hardened into something colder. "Victor's using you to get to me. To Emily."

Mia nodded, miserable. "He called me late yesterday. Said there'd been a break-in at the mill that had raised questions about you. Wanted me to keep eyes on you."

Theresa's mind raced. The ledger, the planner, Claire Pike's whisper. Victor was closing in.

She knelt, took Mia's hands. "No more secrets. We end this together."

Mia's tears slowed. "What do we do?"

Theresa opened the *EMILY – DO NOT DELETE* folder on her phone. "We give Victor what he wants. A whole truckload of proof he can't ignore."

She drafted an email from Mia's account, addressed to Victor.

Subject line: *Payment Plan Update*

"Mr. Johnson,

I can't pay this month. But I have something better. Meet me at the daycare tonight, 10 p.m. Alone. I'll have what you're looking for.

—M. Torres"

She hit Send before Mia could protest.

Alex's eyes widened. "You're baiting him."

"Controlled burn, remember?" Theresa said. "We control the fire this time."

They spent the day planning. Theresa was glad it was Saturday, and they had the time. Alex adjusted the cottage's security cameras so they'd capture footage from every angle, covering every shadow. Theresa made copies of the ledger page, the planner entry, and photos of the cuff link. Mia baked apology cookies like a peace offering to the universe. Milo was subdued, only responding to questions with a dinosaur rawr.

With a quarter hour to go, the cottage was dark, nanny cams rolling. Theresa hid in the supply closet with Alex, laptop open to the feeds. Mia sat on the circle-time rug, Theresa's hoodie on, a decoy folder in her lap. Milo had been picked up by his grandmother two hours ago.

Victor arrived on time, Ray a step behind. No SUV in sight this time, just the tame black sedan parked across the street.

Theresa watched on the teddy bear cam. Victor's charm was gone, replaced by something feral.

"Where is it?" he demanded.

Mia's voice shook but held. "First, you forgive Javi's debt. In writing."

Victor laughed. "You think you're in a position to negotiate?"

Ray cracked his knuckles. "Clock's ticking, sweetheart."

Mia slid a folder across the rug. "Everything. Ledger, planner, cuff link. Enough to bury you."

Victor opened it, face paling. Ray leaned over his shoulder. Theresa saw the moment realization hit, because in one instant Victor's jaw clenched, and in the next Ray's scar twitched.

"You little—" Victor lunged.

Theresa burst from the closet, Alex behind her with a flashlight like a baton.

"Police are on their way," she informed them. "Touch her, and every camera in this room uploads to the cloud."

Victor froze. Ray's hand went to his waistband, where Theresa saw the bulge of a gun.

Alex stepped forward. "Don't. You're on camera. Smile."

The standoff lasted ten seconds that felt like years. Sirens wailed in the distance, real ones. Knowing their response time was about fifteen minutes, Theresa had called them beforehand, reporting a possible break-in.

Victor's eyes darted to the windows. "This isn't over."

He and Ray bolted. The sedan peeled away just before patrol cars screeched up.

Officer Daniels climbed out, looking annoyed. "Ms. Daye. Again."

Theresa handed him the folder with the original documents. "Evidence. Murder, embezzlement, extortion. Call it in."

Daniels flipped through the pages, annoyance shifting to grim focus. "You should've come to us sooner."

"I did," Theresa said. "You told me to change my passwords."

Daniels had the grace to look ashamed.

Mia was shaking, wrapped in a blanket Alex had found in the reading nook. Theresa sat beside her.

"I'm sorry," Mia whispered.

Theresa hugged her. "We're family. Family fights dirty, then forgives."

The police took statements for hours. Victor and Ray were gone. The sedan was found abandoned next to the river, with no sign of them. But the evidence was ironclad.

Theresa locked the cottage at dawn, the rainbow door catching the first light. She texted Claire Pike using the information Alex had found.

This is Theresa Daye. Can you meet me for coffee? I have something that belongs to Leonard.

Claire replied instantly: *Maple Café. 8 a.m.*

Theresa looked at Mia and Alex, exhausted but unbroken.

"Phase two," she said.

The blog was dead. The monsters were cornered.

And Theresa Daye, who had turned into a protector, sleuth, and keeper of red-crayon cliffs, was just getting started.

Chapter Eleven

Theresa arrived at the café clutching a manila envelope like a life raft. The air smelled of rich coffee with overtones of dark chocolate. Theresa knew from experience that the coffee would taste even better.

Claire Pike was already in the corner booth, nursing black coffee, eyes bloodshot but sharp. She looked like someone who'd slept in her clothes and hadn't decided whether to keep living in them.

Theresa slid in opposite her. "Thank you for coming."

Claire's fingers drummed the table. "You said you had something of Leonard's."

Theresa opened the envelope, slid out the sandwich bag with the cuff link.

Claire's breath hitched. "Where did you—"

"Emily's backpack." Theresa said quietly. "She saw everything."

Claire's hand covered her mouth. A tear slipped, unacknowledged. "They told me it was an accident. But I knew. I *knew*."

Theresa laid the ledger page beside the cuff link. "Victor embezzled Leonard's share. This is the transfer for his entire net worth, the day after he died."

Claire traced the numbers with a trembling finger. "He was going to the police. Had proof on a flash drive. Victor invited him over to 'talk numbers.'"

Theresa's throat tightened. "Emily was there."

Claire closed her eyes. "She's eight."

"I know." Theresa hesitated, then added, "I need help understanding what she saw. There are drawings...I can't show the originals. Too risky. But I made copies."

Claire nodded, steel returning to her spine. "Take me to them."

They left the café. Theresa drove, Claire silent in the passenger seat, cuff link clenched tightly in her fist. The daycare was closed, the rainbow door locked tight. Theresa let them in the back way, past the tire swing that squeaked even without wind.

Inside, the cottage felt haunted with dim sunlight slanting through dust motes, the faint scent of yesterday's crayons in the air. Theresa led Claire to the art closet, a walk-in space lined with shelves of construction paper, glitter jars, and labeled bins of *POM-POMS, GOOGLY EYES, RECYCLED BOTTLE CAPS*. Emily's folder was on the top shelf, marked in Theresa's neat block letters: *JOHNSON, E. – DO NOT DISCARD.*

Theresa pulled it down, heart pounding. She'd spent last night with Alex's scanner, making high-res copies of every drawing, then hiding the originals in a lockbox bolted to her apartment floor. Paranoia, maybe. Survival, definitely.

She handed Claire the copies. Claire spread them on the craft table like tarot cards.

The first one was the red cliff, the falling figure, the faceless witness.

The second showed a stick-house with a basement door, a red *X* over it.

The third was an intricate maze so dense it looked like a bruise, Emily's name in the center.

Claire's breath shook. "She's trapping it. The memory. In lines."

Theresa's phone buzzed. She glanced at the screen. It was Dr. Macy confirming a 10:00 a.m. emergency appointment. She'd called the child psychologist yesterday, claiming a "hypothetical trauma case." Dr. Macy had agreed to see her off the books, no names.

"I have to go, but I'll be back soon," Theresa said. "Will you—"

"Stay?" Claire finished. "Try and stop me."

Theresa left Claire with the copies and a fresh pot of coffee, then drove to Dr. Macy's office, which was inside a converted Victorian on Oak Street, porch swing creaking, wind chimes singing. The waiting room held an axolotl housed in a fish tank gurgling in the corner.

Dr. Macy was mid-forties, with warm brown skin and her hair in a sleek bun. She ushered Theresa into a sunlit room with beanbags, a sand tray, and a wall of fidget toys.

"No child today?" Dr. Macy asked.

Theresa handed over the envelope of copies. "Hypothetical, as I mentioned. But urgent."

Dr. Macy spread the drawings out on a low table, expression shifting from curious to grave. She studied the red cliff first.

"Tell me what you see," Theresa prompted.

Dr. Macy traced the falling figure with a finger. "The red figure is falling *backward* with their arms out, not reaching forward. That suggests loss of balance from behind, not a leap or slip. And the perspective..." She tapped the witness figure at the cliff's edge. "Drawn from above. The child was likely on stairs, looking down."

Theresa's pulse thrummed. "She saw a push."

"Possibly." Dr. Macy moved to the basement drawing. "The *X* over the door is a classic trauma symbol. 'Do not enter.' The memory is locked, but leaking through." She flipped to the maze. "This is containment.

The child is trying to control the uncontrollable by building walls around it."

Theresa swallowed. "She's eight."

Dr. Macy's eyes softened. "Trauma doesn't care about age. But children are resilient. With safety, trust, and time, she'll redraw the story."

Theresa took notes on her phone, hands steady now. "What should I do?"

"Keep her routine. Let her draw, but don't force. Watch for regression like bedwetting, or nightmares. And if she discloses, believe her. No matter how impossible it sounds."

Theresa thanked her, paid in cash, and left with a sense of confidence and safety. Outside, the wind had picked up, rattling the wind chimes like warning bells.

She drove back to the cottage, mind racing. Claire was still in the art closet, copies spread out like a map. She looked up when Theresa entered.

"Stairs," Claire said. "The house basement has a landing halfway down. Leonard could've been pushed from there, while Emily could have hidden in the doorway."

Theresa nodded. "Dr. Macy confirmed it."

Claire's jaw set. "We get her out. Today."

Theresa's phone buzzed, this time from Alex. *Victor's truck spotted at the mill. Ray's with him. Moving fast.*

Theresa texted back. *Cottage. Now. Bring the lockbox key.*

Claire gathered the copies. "I'll take these to my lawyer. He's been building a civil case for wrongful death. This is the push we need."

Theresa hesitated. "Victor's desperate. If he thinks we have the original drawings—"

"He won't," Claire said. "Not yet. He'll assume you'll have given them to the police, because if the tables were turned, that's what he would have done."

Theresa locked up and drove Claire back to her car, then returned alone. The cottage felt too quiet, the rainbow door mocking her with its cheer.

She opened the art closet and realized something was off. The *POM-POMS* bin was on the wrong shelf. The *GOOGLY EYES* jar had been moved.

Theresa's heart slammed against her rib cage. She pulled out the step stool, reached for Emily's folder.

Gone.

She tore through the closet, clearing shelves, bins, the craft table. Construction paper drifted like snow to the floor. Glitter exploded like shrapnel. The folder was nowhere.

A break-in. In the scant minutes the business was unoccupied while she dropped Claire off.

Theresa's rage ignited, white-hot. She grabbed her phone and opened the nanny-cam app. The teddy bear in the playroom stared back, feed live, but the art closet had no camera. She'd planned to install one today.

She called Alex. "They took Emily's folder. The copies we made of everything."

"We gave the original business documents to the police, and still have the drawings." Alex's voice was grim. "I'm two minutes out."

He arrived with a duffel bag and a determined face. Inside was a new nanny cam, another teddy bear, HD, motion-activated, with cloud backup. He installed it in the art closet in under five minutes, hidden among stuffed animals on the top shelf.

"Night vision, audio, thirty-day loop," he said. "If they come back, we'll have them."

Theresa's hands shook as she helped him. "They know we're close."

Alex met her eyes. "Then we get closer."

They spent the afternoon fortifying the cottage with new deadbolts, window locks, and a motion sensor on the back door. Mia arrived midafternoon, eyes puffy from crying, carrying more apology cookies and a bottle of wine.

"I heard," she said. "I'm so sorry."

Theresa hugged her as she shooed her back out the door. "Mia, don't worry about it. We're way past sorry. We're in war mode."

They reviewed the nanny-cam feeds from earlier that day. The smoke detector and the clock cameras had caught motion in the playroom. It was Ray in a black cap, his signature scar clearly visible. He moved like he knew the layout, heading straight to the art closet. A few moments later, he left with Emily's folder tucked under his arm.

Theresa's rage hardened into resolve. She opened her laptop and created a new encrypted folder: *EVIDENCE – FINAL*. She uploaded the nanny-cam clip, Dr. Macy's notes, the cuff link photos, pictures of the ledger page, and images of the planner. Then she emailed it to herself, Alex, Claire, and, after a moment's hesitation, Officer Daniels, with the subject line *EMILY JOHNSON – CHILD ENDANGERMENT*.

A few minutes after she'd hit Send, Victor called the cottage line. Theresa let it ring twice, then answered on speaker.

"Theresa," he said, voice smooth as oil. "Emily left her unicorn notebook again. I'll swing by."

"No, she didn't," Theresa said. "You're not welcome."

A pause. "You're making this difficult."

"You made it lethal."

Victor's charm cracked. "You have no idea what you're holding."

"I have everything," Theresa said. "And it's going to the DA tomorrow."

She hung up before he could reply.

Alex stared at her. "You just declared war."

"Good," Theresa said. "Let him come."

They locked the cottage as it got dark outside, leaving the teddy bear's eyes glinting in the dark. Theresa drove home with Alex following, the wine and cookies untouched. At her apartment, she gave Alex a wave, then bolted the door, wedged the chair under the knob, and opened the lockbox.

The original drawings were still there. Still safe. She'd moved them to her bedroom floor safe out of an abundance of caution, leaving only a decoy folder in the closet. Her paranoia had paid off.

She texted Claire *DA tomorrow?*

Claire responded, *8 a.m. My lawyer's office. Bring coffee.*

Theresa set her alarm, then sat at her window. At 11:12 p.m., a black SUV slowly drove past.

This time, she smiled.

The teddy bear was watching.

And tomorrow, the monsters would learn what happened when you stole from a daycare teacher's art closet.

***

Theresa's apartment was a fortress of locked doors and silent nanny-cam feeds, but by 11:30 p.m., the walls felt like they were closing in. She'd texted Alex a quarter hour ago, right after the SUV drove by.

I need to go to Riverbend Lane. Let me know if you want to come along. If so, bring binoculars.

Now, Alex's truck idled outside, engine a low growl against the November chill.

She slipped out in black jeans, hoodie, and the kind of determination that didn't need coffee. Alex handed her a thermos anyway. It was filled with cocoa, extra marshmallows, and a dangerous attraction, because he was Alex, and she was beginning to see beyond the surface of him.

"You meant Victor's house," he said, nodding toward the GPS. "I drove past it earlier. 1427 Riverbend. Glass box on the hill. His lights were still on."

They drove in silence, Willow Creek's streets empty except for the occasional raccoon rooting through trash. The truck's cab smelled of pine air freshener and the addictive cocoa. Theresa clutched the binoculars in both hands like a weapon.

Riverbend Lane wound around and up the hillside, sterile and shiny mansions set back from the road like sleeping giants. Victor's house was all sharp angles and floor-to-ceiling windows, lit from within like a lantern. Ray's silhouette was visible through the glass front door. An older truck, very much beat-up, sat in the driveway.

Alex killed the headlights two houses down and quietly parked under a canopy of oaks. "We're ghosts," he whispered.

They rolled the windows down an inch. Cold air slipped in, carrying the distant rush of the river. Theresa adjusted the binoculars. Up the street, captured in the tiny pictures viewable from within the binoculars, Victor paced the living room, phone to his ear. Ray stood by the fireplace, arms crossed, scar catching the light.

Alex leaned across Theresa and opened the glove box. He pulled what looked kind of like an umbrella from inside, then quickly opened it into a half circle.

"What is that?" She stared at him through the darkness, wondering if a blush worked its way up his throat.

"It's a parabolic microphone. You can find lots of things in the library's lost-and-found box." He plugged a cord into his phone, then held it up and pointed it at the house.

"How do you manage to come up with the precise thing needed every time?" Theresa felt her own cheeks flushing. "I want to call bogus on the 'lost and found,' but I can't."

He seemed to know exactly how it worked. Now it, and he, felt like a lifeline. He aimed it toward the house and pulled out a pair of Bluetooth earbuds. They each took one.

Victor's voice crackled through, tinny but clear.

"—can't find the folder. Ray says the daycare was clean."

Ray's reply was a growl. "If that kid talks, we're done."

Theresa's breath fogged the window. She wrote the words in her phone notes, fingers trembling.

Victor ignored Ray and laughed into the phone, sharp and ugly. "Yeah, right. I can't believe my sister saddled me with her. But she's eight. Who'd believe her? I gotta go." His hand dropped down to his side.

Ray said, "I'll tell you who believes her. That teacher does. And the widow. They're circling."

Victor stopped pacing. "Then we clip the circle. Starting with the kid."

Theresa's blood turned to ice. Alex's hand found hers in the dark, and he squeezed once, tightly.

They listened for twenty more minutes of Victor ranting about offshore accounts, amid Ray suggesting "an accident at the mill." Emily's name came up three times, each mention a knife twist to Theresa's heart.

Later, after what seemed a lifetime, the lights in the house dimmed. The truck's back gate opened, and Ray loaded something heavy. Victor followed, coat flapping.

Alex started the truck. "We follow."

They tailed at a distance, headlights off, the truck's taillights twin red eyes. It wound down the hill, past the festival grounds now dark and empty, toward the river. The old mill loomed ahead, its silhouette jagged against the moon.

Victor parked behind the building. Ray got out, flashlight sweeping the area. Alex cut the engine, and they coasted to a stop behind a dumpster.

Theresa's heart hammered. "They're destroying evidence."

Alex grabbed the binoculars. "Or planting it."

They watched Ray carry a duffel into the mill. Victor stayed by the truck, smoking, phone glowing. Theresa snapped photos—license plate, Ray's scar, the duffel's bulge.

After about an hour, Ray emerged empty-handed. They drove off.

Alex exhaled. "We need to see what they left."

Theresa was already out of the truck, flashlight in hand. The mill's service gate was still unlocked, and she thanked Ray's carelessness in not checking it. Inside, the air was thick with dust and the smell of rust. Their footsteps echoed.

They found the duffel on the second floor, zipped but not locked. Inside was Emily's missing art folder, the pages shredded into confetti. A flash drive. A single gold cuff link—Leonard's match.

Theresa's voice nearly failed her, the idea of Emily's uncle putting her in peril was infuriating. "They're planning for Emily to be a witness. Planting evidence to discredit her if she talks."

Alex pocketed the flash drive. "We take this to Claire. Now."

"And this." Theresa grabbed the cuff link. "This is Claire's too."

They were back in the truck within thirty minutes, the mill shrinking in the rearview. Theresa's hands shook as she texted Claire. *Are you available to meet? We have more information.*

Claire's reply was quick. *Door's open. Is this a lawyerly kind of meeting?*

Could become such.

Roger that.

They drove to Maple Lane, a quiet street of dark bungalows except for one, its porch light glowing. Claire waited on her steps, robe shrugged on over pajamas, eyes fierce. Her lawyer, Mr. Hargrove—fortunately no relation to the PTA tyrant—was already inside, tie askew. His familiarity with Claire's house was reflected in the robust smell of coffee brewing.

Theresa laid out the night's haul, one piece at a time. The shredded drawings, the cuff link, the flash drive. Alex plugged it into Hargrove's laptop.

Files loaded in saved folders on the flash drive, including bank transfers, emails between Victor and an offshore account service, a video file dated March 14.

Hargrove clicked Play.

Grainy security footage—Victor's basement, time-stamped 9:03 p.m. Leonard entered through the doorway to the main level, planner in hand. Victor followed. Words were exchanged, too low to hear. Then Victor's hand on Leonard's back—a shove. Leonard stumbled, arms windmi ling. He fell backward down the stairs, a sickening crack as his head hit the landing.

Emily's small face appeared at the top of the stairs, unicorn notebook clutcned to her chest. She froze, then ran.

The video cut to b'ack.

Claire's sob broke the silence. "That's my husband."

Hargrove's voice was steel. "This is murder. We go to the DA at dawn."

"But why would they have planted evidence that clearly proves Victor's the killer? They were talking about eliminating Emily as a witness." Theresa shook her head. "Unless Ray put the wrong drive in the bag. Or maybe Ray's going to throw Victor under the bus?"

"Doesn't make sense, that's for sure." Hargrove shrugged. "I'm just pleased you've found so much evidence."

Theresa's phone buzzed, from yet another unknown number. She answered on speaker.

"Hello."

Victor's voice, calm as death. "You have something that belongs to me."

Theresa's grip tightened around the phone. "You mean the video of you pushing Leonard down the stairs?"

Silence. Then he demanded, "Bring it to the mill. Midnight tomorrow. Come alone, or the kid disappears."

The line went dead.

Claire's eyes blazed. "He's bluffing."

"He's cornered," Hargrove said. "Cornered animals bite."

Alex looked at Theresa. "We don't go alone."

Theresa nodded, the plan forming. "We go prepared."

They spent the next hour strategizing, with Hargrove calling in favors with the DA, Claire pulling Leonard's old files, and Alex syncing the flash drive to a cloud no one could touch. He had been a font of information at every turn.

Her heart hurting, Theresa stared at the shredded drawings, Emily's clever and unique mazes reduced to so much confetti.

They left Claire's with a plan. They would meet the DA at 8:00 a.m., then set the trap at the mill. Theresa and Alex drove back to her apartment, the sky lightening to bruised purple.

In the parking lot, under a flickering streetlamp, Alex cut the engine. The silence was heavy, electric.

Theresa turned to him. "We're in this together."

He reached across the console and cupped her face. "Always."

The kiss was adreraline and cocoa and fear and hope, rushing through her system all at once. His lips were warm, tasting of marshmallows and the sweetness of chocolate. Theresa's hands fisted in his hoodie, pulling him closer. The world narrowed to the cab of the truck, the hum of the streetlamp, the thud of her heart.

They broke apart, foreheads touching.

"Tomorrow," Alex whispered, "we end this."

Theresa nodded, the taste of him still on her lips. "Tomorrow. We start us."

She watched him drive away, then climbed the stairs to her apartment. The lockbox waited, the nanny cams blinked, and the evidence was ironclad.

Victor thought he was hunting.

He had no idea the prey had teeth.

Chapter Twelve

Theresa woke to the sound of her phone exploding. She'd barely napped, and it was still over an hour before the cottage was due to open. Now, texts, emails, missed calls—dozens of them. The *Kid Quips* blog was dead, but the internet had resurrected it in meme form. A local news station, Channel 7 Action News, had run a segment during the early-morning show: "LOCAL BLOGGER TARGETED? Anonymous Threats Shut Down Popular Kids' Page."

She opened the clip on her laptop, heart in her throat.

A perky reporter stood in front of Sunnybrook Cottage, rainbow door blazing in the background. Theresa's face was blurred in a still from an old blog post, but the daycare sign was crystal clear.

"Willow Creek's beloved 'Miss T' has gone silent after a series of disturbing online threats. Sources say the blog, famous for hilarious kid quotes, may have exposed a child to danger. Parents are asking, is Sunnybrook Cottage safe?"

The segment cut to Mrs. Hargrove, clutching Landon's hand outside the grocery store. "I trusted Miss T with my child's privacy. Now I'm reconsidering."

Theresa's stomach churned. She forwarded the clip to Alex, Claire, and Hargrove with the subject line: *Damage control. NOW.*

Within fifteen minutes, she was at the cottage, unlocking the rainbow door with hands that wouldn't stop shaking. There was paint all over the back window, and the smell of paint was overwhelming, and the nanny cams blinked red—motion detected overnight. She opened the feeds.

After 3:00 a.m., it was Ray again. This time, he'd spray-painted the back window: *KEEP QUIET* in dripping red letters. The teddy bear cam caught him smirking as he left.

Theresa's rage was a living thing. She grabbed paint remover from the supply closet and scrubbed until her arms ached, but the ghost of the words lingered on the glass.

Mia arrived, eyes wide. "T, the parents' group chat is a war zone. Three families already pulled their kids."

Theresa opened the chat on her phone. Messages scrolled like a horror show.

Mrs. Hargrove: *I cannot subject my child to your callous disregard for his safety.*

Mrs. Delgado: *Pulling Priya. Can't risk it.*

Mr. Chen: *Marco's out until this is resolved.*

Mrs. Albert: *Safety first. Sorry, Miss T.*

Theresa's throat closed. She texted the remaining parents. *Cottage closed today for emergency maintenance. Sorry for the late notice. Updates to follow.*

Midmorning, Victor's truck pulled up. Emily tumbled out, unicorn notebook clutched to her chest, braid unraveling and disheveled. Victor followed, his own appearance impeccable, smile lethal.

Theresa met them at the door. "We're closed."

Victor's eyes flicked to the scrubbed window. "Emily forgot something here. And I thought we'd discuss her...adjustment."

Emily's gaze darted inside, then to Theresa. "Miss T?"

Theresa crouched so they were at eye level. "Hey, witchling. Everything okay?"

Emily's lip trembled. Victor's hand settled on her shoulder, that grip again way too tight. "Uncle Victor, I wanna stay with Miss T."

Victor's grip tightened even further. "We're leaving."

Emily screamed. It was a raw, animal sound that shattered the morning, and startled Victor into stillness. She wrenched free, bolted behind Theresa, and latched onto her legs like a barnacle. Theresa wrapped her arm around Emily's poor shoulders, holding her close.

"No! The monsters!" Emily shouted.

Victor's mask slipped as he grabbed the edge of the door. "Emily. Now."

Theresa stood, Emily clinging to her waist. "She's staying with me."

Victor's voice dropped to a hiss. "You're making a mistake."

"Take your hand off the door," Theresa said, voice steel. "Or I call the cops. Again."

Victor's eyes prom sed violence, but the street was awake with neighbors walking dogs, a mail truck idling, and a mom jogging past pushing a stroller. With so many potential witnesses, he stepped back, smile reappearing like a scar. "This isn't over."

He drove off, tires spitting gravel.

Emily was sobbing into Theresa's hoodie. Theresa carried her inside, locked the door, and sat on the circle-time rug. Mia brought juice and a blanket.

"Monsters," Emily whispered. "Uncle Ray said they'd get me if I told "

Theresa's heart cracked. She texted Alex, *Emily's with me. Victor's escalating. I'm taking her to a safe house.*

Alex responded, *My cousin lives in Portland. Let me know if you need anything.*

Theresa looked at Mia. "Pack her a bag. Unicorn notebook, favorite naptime stuffed animal from the stuffies, clothes from the change room for a week."

Mia nodded, eyes wet. "What about the cottage?"

"Closed until Victor's in cuffs."

Theresa opened her laptop and drafted an email to all parents.

Subject line: *Temporary Closure – Safety First*

"Sunnybrook families,

Due to recent threats, the cottage is closed effective immediately. Your children's safety is my priority. Refunds for this week will be processed. I'll update you when it's safe to reopen.

—Miss T"

She hit Send, then called her sister, Lauren, in Eugene. "I need a favor. Big one." She spent only minutes talking before Lauren interrupted her.

"Bring her."

"Emily's my witchling. See you soon, Sis."

By noon, Theresa, Emily, and Mia were in Theresa's car, headed south on the interstate highway. Emily slept in the back, unicorn notebook on her lap, thumb in her mouth, one of those regressions Dr. Macy had warned about. Theresa's eyes flicked to the rearview every handful of seconds, expecting to see the rusty old truck.

They reached Lauren's house, a craftsman bungalow with a tire swing and a golden retriever named Pickles. Lauren met them at the door, arms open. Emily clung to Theresa until Lauren knelt and offered her a sugar cookie shaped like a dinosaur.

"Hi, witchling," Lauren said. "Pickles needs a spell to find his tail. Think you can help?"

Emily managed a nod. Theresa's eyes burned.

Inside, Lauren had set up a guest room with glow stars on the ceiling, a bin of Legos, and a new sketchbook. Emily crawled onto the bed, exhausted.

Theresa tucked her in. "You're safe here. No monsters."

Emily's voice was soft when she asked, "Promise?"

"Cross my heart."

Mia stayed with Emily while Theresa and Lauren talked in the kitchen. Lauren poured wine and Theresa laughed, the sound coming out garbled and choked with tears. "These are real glasses, not daycare sippy cups."

"You're in deep," Lauren said.

"Deeper than the Mariana Trench. I've effectively kidnapped her. If you help me, that puts you in danger too. I'm still going to ask you to give her sanctuary, though." Theresa showed her the flash drive, the cuff link, the nanny-cam clips. "On the way here, I got a call that we were supposed to meet with the DA today, but with me out of town, that had to be pushed off to tomorrow. Victor's cornered."

Lauren's eyes narrowed. "And the kid?"

"Key witness. Victor wants her silenced."

Lauren hugged her. "She stays as long as she needs. You too."

Theresa's phone buzzed with a weighty voicemail from Channel 7 again. "Miss T, care to comment on the closure?"

She ignored it.

Not much later, Alex arrived with Claire and Hargrove. They set up in Lauren's dining room, evidence spread across the table like a war map. Hargrove was working with the DA to get a warrant in progress for murder, embezzlement, and child endangerment.

Claire watched Emily through the cracked bedroom door, drawing mazes in the new sketchbook. "She's braver than all of us."

Theresa's decision crystallized. "Cottage stays closed until he's locked up. Emily stays here. I'll work remotely—blog tips can fund the legal fight."

Alex's hand found hers under the table. "We'll rebuild anything we need to, Theresa. Rainbow door and all."

Theresa looked at the evidence, the team, the sleeping child. The blog was nothing more than backlash and ashes, but the playroom's heart still beat.

She emailed the parents one last time.

"Sunnybrook families,

Update: Sunnybrook is on hiatus, but the kids are my world. When we reopen, it'll be safer, stronger. Thank you for trusting me with your littles.

—Miss T"

She hit Send, then turned off her phone.

Outside, the tree branches swayed in the light breeze that always seemed to exist in Eugene. Inside, Emily dreamed of dinosaurs and safe exits.

And Theresa Daye—former blogger, current guardian—stood watch.

Chapter Thirteen

The Willow Creek Police Station smelled. And the scent wasn't of anything good. It was more like wasted dreams and institutional despair. Theresa arrived in the early morning, her car still warm from the drive back from Eugene. Emily was safe with Pickles and Lauren, plus a full stack of dinosaur stickers. Theresa's heart ached with every mile between them. Claire Pike waited in the lobby, eyes red-rimmed but fierce, Hargrove at her side with a briefcase as thick as a big city telephone book.

Officer Daniels met them at the front desk, looking like he'd slept in his uniform. He may also have been contributing to the olfactory abundance of the squad room. "I've got the interview rooms ready. DA's on her way."

Theresa's pulse thrummed. The evidence—all of it, from the flash drive, cuff link, ledger, and nanny-cam clips—was in a sealed envelope marked *JOHNSON, V. — MURDER*. She handed it over like a grenade.

Daniels led them down a hallway lined with wanted posters and flickering fluorescents. The first room had a label on it that read *CLAIRE PIKE*. The next room was

EVIDENCE REVIEW. There was a third room labeled *HARGROVE.*

*Why would they need a separate room for Claire's lawyer? Unless…*Theresa nearly had a fit of inappropriate giggles, imagining Mrs. Hargrove seated in one of the stiff-backed chairs.

Claire squeezed Theresa's hand, pulling her back to the present. "Let's bury him."

***

Claire sat ramrod straight. Detective Kowalski—who was new to the case, outranked Daniels, and was sharp-eyed, no-nonsense—sat across from her, recorder on.

"Mrs. Pike, walk us through March 14."

Claire's voice didn't waver. "Leonard came home at 6:00 p.m. Said he was meeting Victor at nine to 'settle accounts.' He'd found discrepancies. There were millions of dollars missing. He was leaving me too. I didn't know at the time, but there were divorce papers in his briefcase." She laughed bitterly. "I wouldn't have fought him. The arguments we were having…But I didn't kill him."

Kowalski leaned in. "You were home?"

"Alone. Watched *The Crown* until I got the notification from the sheriff about Leonard's death. Neighbors saw my lights on."

Theresa watched through the one-way glass, Alex beside her. Claire's motive was real—betrayal and humiliation—but her grief was raw, honest.

Kowalski slid the flash drive across the table. "This shows Victor pushing your husband. You recognize the basement?"

Claire's nod was slow. "Our old house. We sold it to Victor last year. He kept the security system."

Hargrove interjected, "My client has no alibi for the push, but she has no access to the house. Victor changed the keys."

Kowalski made a note. "We'll verify."

Claire's eyes shifted to stare at the glass, and Theresa felt the weight of her gaze. "I didn't kill him. But I wish I'd stopped him from going."

The questioning had paused for a few minutes when the inimitable Mrs. Hargrove swept in like a storm cloud in pearls, a young man slouching behind her. According to Kowalski, Dylan was her oldest son, who Theresa had never heard a single whisper of, twenty-two, tattooed, and fresh from a six-month stint for possession. Kowalski made a big deal about separating them, putting Mrs. Hargrove in the now-empty first room and Dylan in the third.

Theresa watched Dylan first. He fidgeted, picking at a scab. Kowalski entered with a file in hand.

"Dylan Hargrove. You threatened Ms. Daye's blog last month. Anonymous comments like 'Ask Maze Girl what Daddy did in the basement.'"

Theresa's mouth dropped open. Kowalski hadn't prepared her for the line of questioning. In all honesty, she didn't know why he was giving her the access he had, but she wasn't going to beg off. The more information she learned meant the more leverage she might have.

Dylan shrugged. "Mom made me. Said the blog was 'inappropriate.' I was bored. She posted funny stuff."

"Your prints were on the spray paint at the daycare. *KEEP QUIET.*"

Dylan paled. "That wasn't me. I was—"

"Video from a security camera," Kowalski said, sliding a still image across the table. Dylan in a gray jumpsuit, time-stamped 2:17 a.m., waving at the camera with a local truck stop in the background. "You were at work. Alibi for that is ironclad. Your access to jail library computers is being traced as we speak. But your prints were still on the paint cans. How do you explain that?"

Mrs. Hargrove burst in, indignant. "My son is *reformed*. How dare you insinuate otherwise. The blog endangered children! It was a menace. The daycare was barely tolerable as it was, then add in the way she made our children out to be the butt of jokes. It shouldn't be allowed."

Theresa's jaw clenched. She was still back at the point in Dylan's responses that told her the on-the-dot subject of his threatening questions was because she'd posted the maze at all. It was just serendipity that it aligned with Victor's harassment. Red herring. Dead end.

Kowalski dismissed them with a warning.

***

Theresa, Alex, Claire, and Hargrove crowded around a monitor. Kowalski plugged in the nanny-cam USB.

The teddy bear feed loaded with detected movement, time-stamped at 2:03 a.m. the night before. Ray, black cap, scar glinting under night vision. He moved through the playroom like a ghost, straight to the nap room. The camera across the hallway caught him standing over the empty mattresses.

He didn't touch anything. Just *looked*. For thirty-seven seconds. Then he left.

Theresa's skin crawled. "He was checking if she was there."

Kowalski's jaw tightened. "Stalking. We'll add it to the warrant."

Claire's voice was ice. "He's hunting my husband's witness."

Ms. Ramirez, the DA, charged into the room like a woman on a mission. She was in her mid-forties, had a body that said she ran regularly, and was dressed in a suit sharp as a blade. She reviewed the flash drive, the ledger, the cuff link, the nanny-cam clip. Her eyes flicked to Theresa.

"You built this case, Ms. Daye. Risked everything."

Theresa's throat tightened. "Emily's eight. She drew cliffs in red crayon. She's smart, and clever, which aren't always a great combination, but with Emily, it just works." She paused. "Am I going to be in trouble for taking her away from her uncle?"

"Doubtful. I will not recommend any action be taken. You'll want to start the process to be her emergency foster home immediately, however. It's best to get those details in place as soon as you can." Ramirez smiled at Theresa. "I know a couple of people, can pull some strings. Leave it to me in the short term, but you'll still have to do the paperwork if you're planning on staying involved."

"She doesn't have anyone else, so I am. I am very much so."

"Okay. Let's get rolling." Ramirez clapped her hands. "Warrants are being signed now. Murder, embezzlement, child endangerment, stalking. We're bringing Johnson in."

Theresa's phone buzzed with a text from Lauren. *Emily drew a new picture. You and her holding hands. Rainbow door in the background.*

Theresa's eyes burned. She showed Claire. Claire's smile was small but real.

***

For the second round of Claire's interview, DA Ramirez joined Detective Kowalski. "Mrs. Pike, the divorce papers. Is it your understanding that Mr. Pike was leaving you for the embezzlement proceeds?"

Claire's laugh was hollow. "He was leaving me for *peace*. I was the one who found the discrepancies. Confronted him. He said Victor would handle it." Her voice cracked. "I should've called the police."

Ramirez slid the mill ledger across. "You knew about Cayman Tide?"

"I suspected. After his death, I found out Leonard kept a second set of books. I have them." Claire opened her purse, pulled a flash drive. "He emailed them to himself the day he died. The subject line said 'if anything happens.'"

Theresa's breath caught. Another nail.

***

Kowalski had a patrol car pick up Dylan Hargrove again. He came accompanied by his mother. She stood behind him, hands on his shoulders as Kowalski played the spray-paint clip. Dylan's bravado crumbled.

"It was Ray," he blurted. "Uncle Ray. Mom's cousin. That paint can is from the shed behind our house, from back when I was tagging things like an idiot. I was afraid of getting in trouble, so I was going to quit messing with the blog, but he offered to pay me more than Mom did. He put money on my commissary account until I got out. Said I needed to help keep the kid quiet."

Mrs. Hargrove gasped. "Dylan!"

Kowalski's eyes narrowed. "Ray Moreau?"

Dylan nodded, clearly miserable. "He's Victor's muscle. Said if I didn't, he'd tell my PO I had weed."

Theresa's rage flared. The PTA tyrant's son, a pawn.

***

Detective Kowalski compiled the timeline.

"March 14:

9:03 p.m.: Leonard entering, planner in hand.

9:03: Victor following.

9:04: The shove.

9:04: Leonard's body hitting the floor.

9:04: Emily's face at the top of the stairs.

9:05–9:30: Victor panics, checks Leonard's pulse, sees Emily flee to her room.

9:30–10:00: Searches for the planner—finds it, realizes Leonard has proof.

10:00–10:30: Calls Ray for cleanup and to help stage the scene, leaves the body for Ray, wipes blood, disables cameras (except the hidden one).

10:30–11:12: Waits for 'accidental' timing.

March 15:

$2.3M transferred to Cayman Tide.

Last 48 hours:

Ray stalks daycare, steals drawings, plants evidence at mill."

Hargrove added, "The DA can do her thing for criminal charges, but we've also got a civil suit ready as soon as the criminal case wraps up. Wrongful death and fraud. Claire will be set for life."

Claire's eyes were dry now. "I don't want his money. I want him in a cage."

Not long later, Kowalski's radio crackled. "Suspect vehicle spotted. Riverbend Lane. Moving in."

Theresa's heart slammed in her chest. She, Alex, Claire, and Hargrove piled into the observation room with DA Ramirez. A monitor showed SWAT vans surrounding Victor's glass house. Victor stepped out, hands up, Ray behind him, scar livid.

Emily's scream echoed in Theresa's memory. The red cliff. The monsters.

Ramirez turned to her. "You did this."

Theresa shook her head. "Emily did. I just believed her."

The arrest played live, and she watched every instant of it. Victor in cuffs, Ray snarling. The rainbow door's ghost lingered in Theresa's mind, waiting to reopen.

She texted Lauren. *It's over. Coming home.*

Lauren: *Emily saved you a cookie. Dinosaur-shaped.*

Theresa smiled, tears falling. The interview rooms emptied. The evidence was filed.

The monsters were caged.

And tomorrow, the cottage would breathe again.

Chapter Fourteen

The rainbow door of Sunnybrook Cottage stood open to the wind, a rare day with no children, no laughter, just the faint smell of bleach from Theresa's frantic scrubbing after the spray-paint incident. She would be reopening the daycare on a limited basis, only the families who'd texted variations of *We trust you, Miss T.* But today was prep day, time for restocking goldfish crackers, sanitizing the sensory table, and baking cookies for the parents who hadn't pulled their kids. Emily and Mia were in the nap room, folding blankets into perfect squares. Alex was due at noon with new window locks.

Theresa stood in the kitchenette, apron dusted with flour, sliding a tray of chocolate chip apologies into the oven. The cottage smelled like comfort, a deliberate antidote to the past week's poison. She'd just set the timer when the front door chimed.

A delivery driver in a brown uniform stood on the porch, holding a pink bakery box tied with twine. "Theresa Daye?"

"That's me."

He thrust the box forward. "From a grateful parent. Said to make sure you got these fresh." A sticker on top read *SWEET RISE BAKERY – THANK YOU, MISS T!*

Theresa's heart warmed. Mr. Delgado was a softy compared to his wife.

She tipped the driver five bucks and carried the box to the counter. Inside was a dozen perfect cookies, each swirled with pink frosting and sprinkles. A note in blocky handwriting was nestled in beside the sweet treats.

"You're the best. The kids are lucky. – A Fan"

She smiled, snapped a photo for the eventual blog relaunch, and took a bite.

The cookie was soft, chocolate melting on her tongue, a faint almond undertone. She ate half, then set the rest aside to share with Mia and Alex.

Ten minutes later, the world tilted.

Theresa was wiping the counter when her vision blurred. The sponge slipped from her fingers. Her knees buckled; she caught the edge of the sink, knuckles white.

"Mia?" Her voice came out slurred.

Mia appeared in the doorway, alarm flashing across her face. "T? You okay?"

Theresa tried to answer. The room spun. She slid to the floor, the tile cold against her cheek. The last thing she saw was the pink box, lid half-open, sprinkles scattered like confetti.

Then darkness.

***

She woke to beeping and the stinging scent of antiseptic. Hospital lights glared overhead. Alex sat beside the bed, holding Theresa's hand like it was the only thing keeping him tethered to earth. His eyes were red-rimmed.

"Hey," he whispered. "Welcome back."

Theresa's throat was sandpaper. "What—"

"Sedative. Mild, but enough to knock you out for four hours. They pumped your stomach." His grip tightened. "The cookies were laced."

"Where's Emily?" She winced but got the question out.

"Lauren came and picked her up a few hours ago. We weren't sure how long you'd need to be in the hospital."

Mia stood at the foot of the bed, arms wrapped around herself. "I called 911. You were... blue."

Theresa's mind raced, sluggish but catching up. The delivery. The note—"A Fan."

"Victor," she croaked.

Alex nodded. "Lab's testing the cookies. Kowalski's on it."

Mia's eyes filled. "There's more." She glanced at Alex, then back. "My brother… Javi. Victor's not just holding his gambling debt. He forced Javi to plant the cookies."

Theresa's heart cracked. "You didn't—"

"I didn't know what he was doing!" Mia's voice broke. "When I called him crying after the ambulance took you away, he said it had been meant to scare you, make you back off. I thought… I thought Javi was out from under Victor. I swear, T, I'd never support—"

Theresa reached for her hand. "I know. We're past blame."

The door opened. Detective Kowalski entered, notebook in hand, expression grim. "Ms. Daye. Glad you're awake. We need your statement."

Theresa recounted the delivery, the cookie, the collapse. Kowalski's pen flew.

"Driver's a ghost," he said. "Fake uniform, stolen van. But the bakery box, it seems that Sweet Rise doesn't do pink frosting. Someone's hunting you."

Theresa's blood ran cold. "Victor. Do we know anything about the person they called 'boss'?"

"Nothing, they claimed they worked alone. That the third person was to throw Leonard off the scent if he got nosey." Kowalski looked frustrated. "I'm going to press them on it again."

"So, what's next? More interviews?"

Kowalski nodded. "It means another active arrest warrant. We're bringing him in again. This is attempted murder."

"Again?" She shook her head slowly. "What does that mean?"

"Means he was out on bail. And that proved to be a nearly deadly mistake by the judge."

He left to coordinate with the DA. Alex stayed, thumb brushing her knuckles. "You scared the hell out of me."

Theresa managed a weak smile. "Takes more than a cookie to stop Miss T."

Mia's phone buzzed. She paled. "It's Lauren."

Theresa's heart stopped. "Emily?"

Mia put it on speaker. Lauren's voice was frantic. "Victor showed up. Said it was a family emergency, took Emily. I tried to stop him, but he had papers, said he was her father. I called the police, but all that did was keep me from letting you know any sooner."

Theresa sat up, IV tugging. "Papers? He's not her father. He's claimed just uncle up to this point."

"Custody addendum," Lauren said. "Looked official. Emily was screaming, T. She didn't want to go."

Alex was already dialing Kowalski.

Theresa's mind raced. Victor had planned this. Put her to sleep by poisoning her, create chaos, snatch Emily while everyone was distracted.

Kowalski burst back in, a nurse on his heels. "We have a BOLO on Victor's truck. Last seen heading north on the main highway."

Theresa ripped the IV from her arm. "I'm coming."

"You're not cleared—" the nurse protested.

Theresa was already swinging her legs over the bed, blood welling on her arm. "Try and stop me."

***

They released her with strict orders to rest and a bottle of anti-nausea pills. Alex drove Theresa's car with Kowalski in the passenger seat, his portable radio crackling with updates Mia sat in back next to Theresa, clutching Emily's unicorn notebook like a talisman.

"Riverbend Lane's empty," Kowalski said. "House cleared. Mill's next."

Theresa's phone buzzed, an unknown number. She answered on speaker.

Victor's voice, calm as death. "You're persistent, Theresa."

"Where's Emily?"

"Safe. For now. Bring the flash drive. Mill. One hour. Alone."

Theresa clenched the phone tighter. "You poisoned me."

"A warning. Next time, it's the kid."

The line went dead.

Kowalski's eyes met hers. "We're not letting you go alone."

Theresa nodded, a plan already forming in her mind. "Then we make him think I am."

***

They reached the mill at dusk, the sky bleeding orange. Kowalski's team set up a perimeter—snipers on the roof, vans hidden in the trees. Theresa wore a wire, a replica flash drive in her pocket. Alex kissed her once, fierce and quick, yet still passionate enough to take her breath away.

"Be careful," he whispered.

Theresa stepped into the open, hands raised. The mill loomed ahead, windows like empty eyes.

Victor waited inside the main floor, Emily clutched to his side. She was pale, eyes wide, but appeared unharmed.

"Flash drive," Victor said.

Theresa tossed it. He caught it one-handed.

"You're done," she said. "The police have everything."

Victor's smile was ice. "They have copies. I have the original witness."

Emily whimpered. Theresa's heart shattered.

Kowalski's voice crackled in her earpiece. "We're in position."

Theresa took a step. "Let her go."

Victor's hand tightened on Emily's shoulder. "One more step and she falls. Like Leonard."

Emily's eyes met Theresa's. She mouthed, "Monsters."

Theresa's rage ignited. She lunged.

Victor shoved Emily toward the stairs. Theresa caught her, rolling to the floor. Gunshots cracked—Kowalski's team breaching. Victor bolted, but Ray was already cuffed outside.

Emily clung to Theresa, sobbing. "You came."

"Always," Theresa whispered. "I will always come for you."

***

They found Victor in the river, trying to swim, a bullet lodged in one hip He was arrested in waist-deep water, cursing. The replica flash drive was recovered, intact.

At the hospital, Emily was checked thoroughly. She was dehydrated and plenty scared, but overall okay.

Lauren arrived, their little reunion complete with tears and hugs.

On a less positive note, Theresa found out that Mia had confessed everything about Javi to Kowalski. Good news, her brother received immunity in exchange for his testimony, so he wouldn't go to jail. Second good news, since Victor agreed to drop Javi's debt for the removal of the extortion charges. *Yay.*

Theresa sat with Emily in the pediatric wing, unicorn notebook open to a new page. Emily drew a rainbow door, her and Theresa holding hands next to it.

"The monsters are gone," Emily said.

Theresa kissed her forehead. "And the cottage is waiting."

The close call had nearly broken them.

But their family, forged in poison and fear, was unbreakable now.

Chapter Fifteen

The Willow Creek Courthouse was a squat brick building with columns that tried too hard, but on this morning, it felt like the center of the universe. Theresa sat in the second row, hands clasped so tight her knuckles blanched. Alex was beside her to the right, steady as always; Claire Pike sat on her left, gripping a tissue like a lifeline. Mia had stayed at the cottage with the kids, saying with half seriousness, "Well, someone has to keep the rainbow door open."

The courtroom smelled of lemon polish, and every wooden surface shined like mirrors. Victor Johnson sat at the defense table in a charcoal suit that cost more than Theresa's car, his charm dialed down to zero. He sat with his head down, a dour expression on his face. Victor had been forced to provide information on the person he'd dubbed the "boss," and the DA's office was reviewing evidence even now. They were holding those cards close to the vest so far, Theresa hadn't heard a sniff of who it was. Ray Moreau was at the other end of the table, hands splayed on the top, scar twitching every time the bailiff moved.

Judge Harlan, a woman with steel-gray hair and zero patience, gaveled the room to order. "People versus Johnson and Moreau. Plea proceedings."

The DA, Ms. Ramirez, stood. "Your Honor, the State has reached agreements. Mr. Johnson pleads guilty to voluntary manslaughter and embezzlement. Twenty-five years, no parole for fifteen. Mr. Moreau pleads guilty to accessory after the fact. Ten years, eligible in seven."

Victor's lawyer, a slick type from Portland whose suit was a duplicate of Victor's, nodded. Victor didn't look back. His empire was ash—the offshore accounts frozen, the mill seized, the black sedan and truck impounded.

Ray's public defender added, "Mr. Moreau has provided full cooperation, including the location of Leonard Pike's second planner."

Judge Harlan's eyes narrowed. "Mr. Moreau, you understand this plea waives your right to trial?"

Ray's voice was gravel. "Yes, ma'am."

The judge looked at Victor. "Mr. Johnson, you also understand this plea waives your right to trial?"

Victor stared at her for a moment, then nodded once. "Yes, Your Honor."

Theresa's breath caught. Twenty-five years. Victor might be seventy when he got out—if he survived prison. Leonard's ghost could rest easy.

The judge turned to the screen at the front of the room. "Before sentencing, we'll now hear a victim impact statement from the child witness via closed-circuit. Bailiff, bring in the feed."

The screen flickered. Emily appeared, sitting in a small room with soft lighting and a beanbag chair. She wore a purple sweater and held the teddy bear nanny cam—Theresa's idea, for comfort. Dr. Macy sat off camera, unseen but present.

Ramirez faced the screen, voice gentle. "Do you still want to do this, Emily?"

Emily nodded, clutching the bear. "I do."

Ramirez gave her a soft smile. "Emily, can you tell us what you saw on March 14?"

Emily's voice was small but clear. "Uncle Victor was yelling at Mr. Pike. Uncle Victor pushed him. Mr. Pike fell down to the basement. He was bleeding. I was scared."

The courtroom was silent. Victor's head bowed while Ray stared blankly at the table.

Ramirez asked, "Did anyone tell you not to tell?"

Emily nodded. "Uncle Victor said monsters would come if I talked, so I didn't tell anyone. I kept seeing it happen, had nightmares. But then Miss T said monsters are allergic to truth. So I told her."

A ripple of soft laughter, then silence. Theresa's eyes burned.

The judge thanked Emily. The feed cut. The plea was accepted. Gavel down.

Outside, the media frenzy waited with cameras, microphones, reporters shouting questions. Theresa slipped out a side door with Alex and Claire, heading toward Kowalski's unmarked sedan.

"Theresa! Miss T! Statement?" a reporter yelled.

Theresa paused at the car. "The kids come first. Always."

She slid inside. The door shut on the noise.

***

Back at Sunnybrook Cottage, the rainbow door gleamed under fresh paint. Theresa had repainted it herself, using a brighter spectrum to erase the spray-painted ghosts. Still, the playroom buzzed with half-capacity joy. Priya was building a block tower, Milo debating whether dinosaurs could fly, and three new kids had transferred from a closed preschool across town.

Mia met Theresa at the door, eyes shining. "Emily's asking for you."

Theresa found her in the art corner, unicorn notebook open. A new drawing showed the courtroom, but with a rainbow arching over the judge's bench. Emily and Theresa were holding hands beneath it.

"The monsters are in jail?" Emily asked.

Theresa knelt beside her. "Locked up tight."

Emily hugged her, teddy bear squished between them. "Can we have circle time?"

Theresa's heart swel ed. "Goldfish crackers and all."

***

That night, after the next to last child left and the cottage was quiet, Theresa opened her laptop. The *Kid Quips* mirror site had been dormant since the goings-on, but the domain still hummed with possibility. She'd transferred the old posts to a private archive—memories, not ammunition.

She created a new post, titled *Some Mazes Have Exits*.

"Hey Quipsters,

Miss T here. It's been a wild ride—monsters, cliffs, and goldfish cracker standoffs. But the playroom is open, the rainbow door shines, and the kids are drawing exits instead of walls.

Emily (aka Maze Girl) taught me that truth is the way out. So here's a new rule—no more anonymized quotes. Just joy, with permission.

Today's quip, from Priya: "Rainbows are bridges for feelings."

The cottage is healing. So are we.

Back soon with more glitter and fewer monsters.

—Miss T"

She hit Publish. Immediately the dashboard lit up. The post had a thousand views in ten minutes, comments disabled for now. Tips trickled in with various amounts of $5, $10, $20. Playground fund.

Alex texted her: *Saw the post. Proud doesn't cover it.*

Claire also texted: *Leonard would've loved this.*

Theresa closed the laptop and stood in the playroom. The teddy bear cam blinked once, then went dark. She'd disabled it. No more secrets.

"Em, you ready to go home?"

Outside, Willow Creek slept under a thin February snow. The cottage stood warm, lights glowing through the rainbow door.

"Coming," came a quiet singsong in response to her question.

Theresa whispered to the quiet, "We made it."

The unraveling threads had woven something stronger.

And tomorrow, even more kids would come.

Chapter Sixteen

The cottage garden bloomed like a promise kept. Spring sun spilled over the new playground. It was filled with swings that soared, a slide painted like a rainbow serpent, a tire swing big enough for three. Theresa had fought for every bolt and beam, but the real miracle was the laughter echoing across the grass.

Sunnybrook Cottage had started up again with only a handful of kids, though they had a growing waitlist for when they finally went back to full capacity. The rainbow door gleamed in the sunshine, no evidence of scars present.

Theresa stood on the porch, coffee in hand, watching Emily chase bubbles with Priya and Milo. The girl's braid bounced, her laughter bright as the dandelions dotting the lawn. No more red cliffs. No more mazes. No more quiet girl sitting alone.

Dr. Macy's office had almost become a second home. They had joint weekly sessions, teddy bear in Emily's lap. She drew rainbows now. They arched over houses, over the cottage, over stick-figure families holding hands.

"Rainbows are exits," she'd told Theresa one afternoon, crayon poised like a wand. "They take you somewhere safe."

Theresa's eyes misted. She sipped her coffee, let the warmth ground her.

Mia appeared at her elbow, apron dusted with flour. "Cookies are cooling. Chocolate chip, extra chips. Emily's request."

Theresa smiled. "You're a saint."

"Second assistant starts Monday," Mia said. "Jasmine. I can't wait. You said she's got an early childhood degree, sings like an angel, and absolutely loves glitter. I'm going to love her."

Theresa nodded. Growth. She'd hired Mia full-time after the case wrapped up, making certain her faith and trust in the woman was visible. Together they could do a lot, but the cottage needed more hands. More hearts.

She'd set blog boundaries, too, promising herself no more late-night posts, no anonymous quotes, and all comments moderated by a crew of volunteer parents. *Kid Quips* was back, but gentler. Safer.

A delivery truck rumbled up the drive. The driver handed Theresa a plain white envelope, no return address. Inside was a cashier's check for $50,000. It was made out to *Sunnybrook Cottage Playground Fund*. A note in elegant script was included in the envelope that simply said "For the children. For the rainbows. — A Friend."

Theresa's breath caught. She knew that handwriting well. This was from Claire Pike, who wanted to remain anonymous as always. The civil suit had settled quietly, turning Leonard's estate over to Claire, including his portion of the company. She'd chosen to give back.

Theresa tucked the check into her pocket, heart full. The playground's final phase, including a sensory garden and musical chimes, was fully and completely funded.

Circle time was called. The kids gathered on the rug, Emily front and center. Theresa read *The Rainbow Fish*, her voice weaving the story of scales and friendship. When the fish shared its last shiny scale, Emily raised her hand.

"Miss T, rainbows are like that. You give pieces away, and everyone gets prettier."

Theresa's throat tightened. "Exactly, witchling."

Snack time followed with the expected goldfish crackers, apple slices, and of course, the chocolate chip cookies. Theresa watched Emily pass the plate first, making sure Milo got the biggest one. Growth in crayon strokes and kind gestures.

Alex arrived at noon, picnic basket in hand. He'd become a fixture at the cottage as story time volunteer, slide monitor, and grandmaster of the tire swing spin. The kids swarmed him, demanding "Uncle Alex" rides. He obliged, laughing, until Emily tugged his sleeve.

"Miss T needs a turn!"

Theresa raised an eyebrow. "I'm good on the ground, thanks."

Alex's eyes twinkled. "Actually, I brought something for circle time."

He pulled a picture book from the basket. It was handmade, with a construction-paper cover, titled *The Cottage That Loved Back*. The kids oohed. And Theresa's curiosity piqued.

They gathered again. Alex read, his voice warm. The story was theirs, with a rainbow door, a brave (carefully anonymized) little girl who drew mazes, a teacher who believed her, and a garden that grew stronger after storms. The illustrations were Emily's—rainbows, dinosaurs, and goldfish crackers.

On the last page, the cottage stood tall, kids playing, a new swing set gleaming. And in the tire swing, two stick figures held hands, one with a braid and one with glasses. Beneath them, in Alex's handwriting: "Will you write the next chapter with me?"

Theresa's heart stuttered. Alex knelt, pulling a small box from his pocket. Inside was a ring, white gold with a tiny rainbow sapphire.

"Theresa Daye," he said, voice steady despite the kids' gasps, "you turned monsters into exits. You made this place a home. Marry me?"

The playroom erupted with cheers, clapping, and Milo yelling, "Say yes, Miss T!"

Tears welled in Theresa's eyes as she nodded, unable to speak, and Alex slipped the ring onto her finger. It fit perfectly.

Emily hugged them both. "Rainbows forever!"

***

Afternoon free play was chaos and joy. Theresa pushed Alex on the tire swing, his laughter mingling with the kids'. Claire arrived unannounced, eyes bright with tears she wouldn't shed.

She smiled. "Leonard would've loved this garden. He always said kids should have places to fly."

Theresa hugged her. "You helped give them wings."

Pickup came too soon. Parents trickled in, oohing over the ring, the playground, the cookies.

Finally the cottage quieted. Theresa locked the rainbow door, but not before snapping a photo of the garden at golden hour, swings still, dandelions glowing. She posted it to *Kid Quips* with the caption:

"Some days are made of hugs and rainbows. Today was one."

Likes poured in. Tips hit $200, which was more than enough for new sensory bins.

Alex waited on the porch, picnic basket repacked with leftovers. "Dinner at my place? I make a mean spaghetti."

Theresa grinned. "Only if Emily can come."

"Already cleared it with her. She's in favor."

They drove to Alex's apartment, which she'd learned was a cozy loft above the library, with books stacked like wallpaper. Emily arrived, dropped off by Mia, unicorn notebook in hand. Dinner was spaghetti and meatballs, garlic bread, and chocolate milk mustaches. Emily drew at the table, placing the three of them under a rainbow, the cottage in the background.

Theresa's ring caught the light. She'd set boundaries, but some things were meant to grow.

Later, tucking Emily in on Alex's couch, Theresa whispered, "Sweet dreams, witchling."

Emily yawned. "No monsters?"

"None left."

Theresa kissed her forehead, then joined Alex on the balcony. The town sparkled below, quiet and safe.

"Next chapter," Alex said, lacing his fingers with hers.

Theresa leaned into him. "With rainbows."

The cottage garden slept under starlight, swings gently swaying. Healing hugs had mended the cracks.

And Miss T, engaged, growing, and unbreakable, would open the rainbow door tomorrow, ready for whatever came next.

Chapter Seventeen

The grand reopening of Sunnybrook Cottage was scheduled for the first Saturday in May, when Willow Creek's cherry blossoms carpeted the streets in pink snow and the air smelled of lilacs and possibility.

Theresa had planned every detail for months, and it had all come together, from the new playground gleaming with fresh paint, the garden bursting with sensory plants, and those glorious rainbow doors repainted in a spectrum so vivid it hurt to look at it directly.

Banners fluttered from the fence, boasting *SUNNYBROOK COTTAGE – STRONGER TOGETHER*. Balloons bobbed in the breeze, tied to every swing and slide.

By opening, the garden was a riot of color and sound. Families poured in, returning kids, new enrollees, and even curious neighbors. The lawn had been transformed with picnic tables draped in checkered cloths, a face-painting station where Jasmine, the new assistant, already a legend, turned Milo into a tiger, and a bounce house shaped like a castle.

A local band—really just three moms with guitars—played kids' songs on the porch. The smell of popcorn and cotton candy drifted from a food truck donated by Sweet Rise Bakery.

Theresa stood at the gate, greeting arrivals with hugs and handshakes. She wore a sundress the color of dandelions, her rainbow sapphire ring catching the light every time she waved. Alex was on the playground, pushing the tire swing for a line of giggling kids. Emily darted between them, unicorn notebook in one hand, a balloon sword in the other, her braid adorned with glitter ribbons.

Claire Pike arrived, understated in linen and sunglasses, carrying a tray of lemonade. She'd become a silent partner in the cottage's rebirth, from the $50,000 for the playground to another $20,000 for art supplies. The donations were all anonymous until Theresa insisted on a plaque: *IN MEMORY OF LEONARD PIKE – FOR THE CHILDREN WHO FLY.*

"Crowd's bigger than expected," Claire said, surveying the chaos. "You'll need a bigger garden."

Theresa laughed. "We'll expand into the back lot. Sensory maze, maybe. Emily's designing it."

The next time Theresa looked to the parking lot, she'd seen the arrival of Mayor Delgado, Mr. D's cousin, mustache trimmed for the occasion. He carried oversized golden scissors, the kind used for photo ops. The kids gathered in a semicircle, Emily front and center with

Priya and Milo. Theresa handed each child a pair of safety scissors tied with rainbow ribbon.

"Ready?" the mayor boomed. "On three. With a one, a two, a *three*!"

The ribbon was a thick satin stripe in every color, and it fell in a flutter of confetti. Cheers erupted. The kids charged the playground, swings creaking, slides whooshing. Theresa's eyes stung. The cottage was whole again.

Mia found her near the sensory table, eyes shining. "T, I need to tell you something."

Theresa braced. Over the past months, Mia's confessions had exhibited a way of upending days. "Go for it."

Mia pulled an envelope from her apron pocket. Inside was a photo of her brother Javi, clean-shaven, standing outside a rehab facility in Arizona. There was also a note in his handwriting: "Ninety days sober. Thank you for believing in second chances."

Theresa's throat tightened. "Mia—"

"There's more." Mia's smile was radiant. "You know that I got promoted. I'm co-director now. Jasmine's full-time, and we, as in you and me, are hiring a third aide. You're not doing this alone anymore."

Theresa hugged her so hard they nearly toppled into the lavender bush. "You earned it. Every glitter stain, every goldfish cracker standoff."

Mia laughed, wiping tears. "Javi's coming home next month. He wants to volunteer here, if he can. He'd do things like fix the fence and maybe build the maze. Redemption looks good on him."

Theresa's heart swelled. The cottage wasn't just hers anymore. It was theirs.

***

The party grew. Parents snapped photos, kids devoured cupcakes frosted with edible glitter, and the band switched to an upbeat song. Theresa's phone buzzed in her pocket with *Kid Quips* notifications. She'd posted a teaser at dawn: "Grand reopening today! Rainbow door swings at 10:00 a.m. Come celebrate exits and entrances."

She opened the dashboard in amazement. The blog had gained over 100,000 subscribers now. The milestone hit like a firework. Tips had poured in overnight to an astonishing $12,547. That was enough for three full scholarships for low-income families, plus new books for the reading nook.

Alex appeared at her side, slipping an arm around her waist. "100K. You broke the internet, Miss T."

Theresa leaned into him. "We did. The kids did."

He kissed her temple. "Scholarship fund's named after Emily, right?"

"Already filed the paperwork. The Maze Girl Scholarship is for kids who find their way out."

Emily ran up, cheeks flushed. "Miss T! The mayor said I get to name the tire swing!"

Theresa crouched. "What's it gonna be, witchling?"

Emily's eyes sparkled. "The Exit Express!"

Theresa laughed until she cried.

***

Afternoon brought games of sack races, three-legged races, and a stubborn piñata shaped like a unicorn that refused to break until Milo took a heroic swing. Claire judged the art contest, awarding blue ribbons to every entrant. The sensory garden—rosemary, mint, lamb's ear—was a hit; kids buried their hands in the soft leaves, giggling at the textures.

As closing time crept up on the party, Theresa gathered everyone for a group photo. The kids stood on the playground, parents behind, the rainbow door framing them like a promise. Alex set the timer and then sprinted into the shot. The camera clicked. A perfect moment, frozen in time.

As the crowd thinned, Theresa found a quiet corner by the new musical chimes. She opened her phone to schedule the scholarship announcements.

Alex found her, eyebrow raised. "Everything okay?"

Theresa smiled, the kind that held both fear and fire. "New chapter."

He followed her gaze to the playground, where Emily was pushing Priya on the Exit Express, their laughter rising like birds.

"Boundaries?" he asked.

"Always." Theresa squeezed his hand. "But some doors you don't close."

The party wound down. Parents collected sleepy kids, sticky with cotton candy and joy. Theresa stood at the gate, waving goodbye, the envelope burning a hole in her pocket.

Mia locked the rainbow door, and they stood for a moment, feeling how the cottage was quiet but alive with echoes of joy. Theresa posted the group photo to *Kid Quips*.

"Hey Quipsters,

We are 100K strong. Scholarships funded. Rainbows planted.

Thank you for believing in exits.

Next adventure? Stay tuned.

—Miss T"

Comments flooded in. They were still set to moderated for now, but the love was evident. Tips hit $15,000 as she watched the site. The comments and tips were a palpable acknowledgment that she'd built something very real here in the daycare.

Alex drove her home, Emily asleep in the back seat, unicorn notebook on her lap. At Theresa's apartment, he carried Emily to the guest room, tucking her in with the teddy bear. Theresa watched from the doorway, ring glinting.

"Co-director Mia, 100K subscribers, a proposal in a picture book," Alex said, joining her. "What's next?"

"Whatever it is, I have a proposal." Theresa's voice was steady. "We do it together. With boundaries. With rainbows."

Alex kissed her, slow and sure. "Team Miss T."

Theresa smiled. The cottage garden slept under a crescent moon, swings waiting for their next rider.

New beginnings weren't endings.

They were exits to somewhere brighter.

Chapter Eighteen

The circle-time rug at Sunnybrook Cottage had never looked more alive. One year after the grand reopening, the playroom glowed with late-May sunlight slanting through windows washed clean of every ghost. The rainbow door stood open to the garden, where the sensory maze, following Emily's design, twisted through rosemary and mint like a living drawing. The cottage hummed with twenty kids, two assistants, and the kind of laughter that stitched scars into stories.

Theresa sat cross-legged at the head of the rug, sundress patterned with tiny goldfish crackers, her wedding ring catching the light every time she turned a page of *The Day the Crayons Quit.*

Alex leaned against the bookshelf, arms crossed, grinning like he still couldn't believe this was his life. Mia, nameplate gleaming on the office door, passed out juice boxes. Jasmine led a quiet game of patty-cake with the toddlers in the corner.

The newest kid, a four-year-old named Leo with a mop of curls and a superhero cape made from a dish towel, raised his hand so high he nearly toppled.

"Miss T! My cat's a secret agent!"

Theresa closed the book, giving him her full attention. "Tell me everything, Agent Leo."

Leo's eyes went wide. "He wears sunglasses at night. And he steals my dad's socks to send coded messages!"

The rug erupted in giggles, gasps, and Milo insisting his goldfish was the cat's handler. Theresa let the chaos bloom, her heart so full it ached. This was the epilogue she'd fought for. Ordinary magic, with no cliffs in sight.

Circle time ended with the cleanup song, off-key and glorious. Theresa helped Leo tie his cape properly, then sent the kids to free play. The garden called, and the Exit Express tire swing needed testing.

***

The wedding had been six months ago, a crisp afternoon in the cottage garden. Theresa had insisted on keeping it small, with only thirty guests, fairy lights strung through the sensory maze, and the rainbow door as backdrop. Alex had worn a navy suit with a pocket square printed with tiny unicorns—Emily's choice. Theresa's dress was simple lace, veil replaced by a crown of daisies woven by Priya's mom.

Mia had gotten ordained online for twenty-five dollars and a multiple-choice quiz. She stood at the altar, in front of a beautiful wooden arch Claire had built from reclaimed mill beams, and cleared her throat.

"Friends, family, and goldfish crackers, we're here to witness the two people who turned monsters into exits choose each other, every day."

Theresa's vows were short. "You believed in rainbows when I saw only storms. I choose you, Alex. Always."

Alex's voice cracked. "You taught me that bravery looks like glitter and grit. I choose you, Theresa. Forever."

Emily, flower girl and ring bearer, marched down the aisle with the seriousness of a knight, unicorn notebook tucked under one arm. She'd drawn their rings on the inside cover—hearts intertwined with rainbows. When Mia asked for the rings, Emily had opened the notebook, revealing two simple bands nestled in a crayon pocket. A secret project she'd worked on with her Aunt Lauren.

They'd kissed under a shower of biodegradable confetti, which was Jasmine's very good idea. The kids cheered. Milo yelled, "Now we get cake!"

And they did—chocolate with rainbow sprinkles, baked by Mia and Javi, who'd come home from rehab sober and steady, apron tied with pride. The wedding truly had been a group project of the best kind.

Claire had cried through the whole ceremony, then danced with Kowalski to "At Last." The cottage garden had never felt more like home.

***

Summer brought acceptance letters. Emily, now nine, clutched the envelope from Willow Creek Arts Camp with trembling hands. Theresa opened it with her in the reading nook, surrounded by stuffed animals and the faint smell of rosemary from the garden.

"Dear Emily Johnson," Theresa read, "we are thrilled to offer you a full scholarship to our Young Artists Program…"

Emily squealed, launching into Theresa's arms. "I get to paint murals! And sculpt! And there's a lake!"

Theresa's eyes burned. The Maze Girl Scholarship had funded three kids this year, but Emily's talent had earned her spot. Dr. Macy had signed off. As far as she was concerned, unless there was a regression, for now Emily's therapy was complete, all nightmares gone. Emily still drew rainbows, but now they arched over cities, over oceans, over futures.

That afternoon, Emily presented Theresa with a card, construction paper folded with care, cover illustrated with the cottage, the garden, the Exit Express. Inside, in purple marker, was a carefully handwritten note:

"Thank you, Miss T, for believing my drawings. You made the monsters small. Love, Emily (Age 9, Artist)"

Theresa tucked it into the frame above her desk, next to the wedding photo and the mayor's ribbon-cutting scissors.

***

The last day of the school year arrived with a heat shimmer and the promise of popsicles. Theresa locked the cottage after the final pickup. It felt odd, with the garden quiet and all the swings still. The kids were gone, all set for their sleepovers, grandparents, and the sweet exhaustion of summer's edge. Emily was outside with Alex. Mia and Jasmine had left for the weekend, with Javi promising to fix the wobbly slide on Monday.

Theresa stood alone in the playroom, the rainbow door framing the garden like a painting. She saw an envelope tucked under the edge of a box of markers. Plain white, no address, her name typed in block letters.

She opened it, heart skipping.

Inside was a single sheet of heavy paper, folded once. The message was handwritten in sharp, slanted ink.

"Heard you solve mysteries, Miss T.

My nephew's drawings are wrong. Too many shadows.

Can you help?

— A Parent"

No signature. No contact info. Just a phone number scrawled at the bottom.

Theresa's pulse quickened. The cottage was safe. The monsters were caged. But shadows lingered in other playrooms, other gardens.

She slipped the note into her pocket, the weight of it familiar. Then she opened her laptop one last time, the *Kid Quips* dashboard glowing. The blog now had 250,114 subscribers. Tips from the blog helped build the maze, funded scholarships, and bought new crayons by the crate. The blog was gentle now, with only weekly posts, parent-approved quotes, and comments moderated with love.

She drafted the final entry of the season.

Title: *The Best Stories End with Hugs*

"Hey Quipsters,

One year ago, we reopened with balloons and hope. Today, the garden laughs, the swings soar, and a new kid swears his cat's a spy.

Emily's off to art camp, Mia's co-director, Javi's building mazes, and Alex still pushes the tire swing like a pro.

Today's quip, from Leo, is "Secret agents need naps too."

The cottage closes for summer break. We'll be back in August, with taller slides, fresher paint, and the same rainbow door.

Thank you for every hug, every tip, and every exit you helped us find.

—Miss T (and the whole Sunnybrook family)"

She scheduled it for 8:00 a.m., then closed the laptop. The playroom was already tidy, cubbies sanitized, books shelved, and discarded goldfish crackers swept into the trash.

Theresa stepped outside, the garden bathed in golden hour. The Exit Express creaked gently in the breeze. She locked the rainbow door, the paint gleaming like it had the day she'd repainted it—brighter, bolder, unbreakable.

Alex waited in his truck, Emily in the back seat with a popsicle and her camp backpack. "Ready, Mrs. Daye-Reed?"

Theresa slid into the passenger seat, her ring catching the light. "Born ready."

He stared at her for a moment, head tilted to the side. "What's happened?"

Theresa pulled the envelope from her pocket and showed him the note.

His eyes widened. "Another mystery?"

"Maybe." Theresa's voice was steady. "But this time, we do it together. With boundaries. With rainbows."

Alex kissed her, slow and sure. "Team Miss T."

Theresa texted the number from the note. *Tell me about the shadows.*

The reply came instantly. *Tomorrow. Coffee in town.*

They drove into the sunset, the cottage shrinking in the rearview. The rainbow door was locked, but not forever.

Laughter would return in August, and it would ring out louder, brighter, with new agents and more vivid rainbows.

And Miss T—wife, guardian, keeper of exits—would be waiting, arms open, heart full.

The best stories, after all, ended with hugs.

The End

ABOUT THE AUTHOR

Raised in the south, *Wall Street Journal* and *USA Today* bestselling author MariaLisa deMora learned about the magic of books at an early age. Every summer, she would spend hours in the local library, devouring books of every genre. Self-described as a book-a-holic, she says "I've always loved to read, but then I discovered writing, and found I adored that, too. For reading...if nothing else is available, I've been known to read the back of the cereal box."

Also by MariaLisa deMora

Alace Sweets

A dark thriller, this book is not a light read. Filled with edge-of-your-seat suspense, this intense story commands the reader's attention as it drives towards the explosive ending. Alace Sweets is a vigilante serial killer, with everything that implies and is sure to trip all your triggers. Be ready.

At seventeen, Alace Sweets turned a corner in her life, taking the wrong shortcut home from school.

Resisting the harsh knowledge her attackers will never be made to pay for their actions, Alace takes a stand. Justice must be served, and if fate's scales are out of balance, she's determined to set things right as best she can.

When the laws of men fail, the rules of Alace prevail.

5-Star Reviews for Alace Sweets

"deMora has a superb story-line and exceptional character development. All of her characters have such depth that will intrigue the reader..."

~Turning Another Page

"Hot, sweet, dark thriller."

~Beth D

"It will keep you on the edge of your seat and give you chills."

~Escape Reality Book Blog

"From the first page [deMora] pulls you into the world she has created and you do not even try to escape..."

~Little Shop of Readers Blog

"A must read for all those dark, gritty romance fans out there."

~Sweet & Spicy Reads

"You will find yourself so drawn into the story that the outside world is blocked out and your locking the doors and turning on all the lights."

~Danena F

"Don't judge me for bonding with a vigilante serial killer, she's more than what she does."

~iScream Books

"Thrilling...chilling...full of suspense, nail biting edge of your seat excitement."

~Tracey H

"Every time MariaLisa deMora picks up her pen (or opens her computer), she creates characters you want to believe in."

~Gail S

"Intriguing dark storyline, beautiful love story and nail-biting conclusion, what more could a reader ask for?"

~Manda M

"This book takes you a dark and twisted ride that is gripping…"

~Renee Entress' Blog

"This book is dark and gr tty and I literally had to take a day off from reading it because it's that intense."

~My Girlfriend's Couch

"This is my favourite book so far from this author … I recommend this book if you enjoy dark romantic thrillers."

~Cheekypee Reads and Reviews

"There's not enough stars to give this book and 5 just doesn't really do it just ce!"

~DeLane C

"I couldn't put this book down from page one! Tried to stop & go to bed but couldn't sleep thinking about Alace and got up & finished the book."

~Debbie M

"MariaLisa DeMora, wordsmith that she is, made this a story of the enlighter ment of a woman and finding love in a life where she has had none."

~Kat W

"Whatever deep dar‹ trench [deMora] pulled a character like Alace ‡rom should be revisited again and often."

~Confessions of a Serial Reader

ADDITIONAL SERIES AND BOOKS

Please note that books in a series frequently feature characters from additional books within that series. If series books are read out of order, readers will twig to spoilers for the other books, so going back to read the skipped titles won't have the same angsty reveals.

Rebel Wayfarers MC series:

Mica, #1
A Sweet & Merry Christmas, #1.5
Slate, #2
Bear, #3
Jase, #4
Gunny, #5
Mason, #6
Hoss, #7
Harddrive Holidays, #7.5
Duck, #8
Biker Chick Campout, #8.5
Watcher, #9
A Kiss to Keep You, #9.25
Gun Totin' Annie, #9.5
Secret Santa, #9.75
Bones, #10
Gunny's Pups, #10.25
Never Settle, #10.5
Not Even A Mouse, #10.75
Fury, #11
Christmas Doings, #11.25
Gypsy's Lady, #11.5
Cassie, #12
Road Runner's Ride, #12.5

Occupy Yourself band series:

Born Into Trouble, #1
Grace In Motion, #2 (TBD)
What They Say, #3 (TBD)

Neither This, Nor That MC series:

This Is the Route Of Twisted Pain, #1
Treading the Trcitor's Path: Out Bad, #2
Shelter My Heart, #3
Trapped by Fate on Reckless Roads, #4
Tarnished Lies and Dead Ends, #5

Rebel Wayfarers crossover stories:

Going Down Easy
No Man's Land
In Search of Solace
Puppy Love
Steel and Swagger

Mayhan Bucklers MC series:

Most Rikki-Tik, #1
Mad Minute, #2
Pucker Factor, #3
Boocoo Dinky Dau, #4

Borderline Freaks MC series:

Service and Sacrifice, #1
More Than Enough, #2
Lack of Inbetween, #3
See You in Valhalla, #4

Alace Sweets series:

Alace Sweets, #1
Seeking Worthy Pursuits, #2
Embarrassment of Monsters, #3
All the Broken Rules, #4

With My Whole Heart series:

With My Whole Heart, #1
Bet On Us, #2

**If You Could Change One Thing:
Tangled Fates Stories**

There Are Limits, #1
Rules Are Rules, #2
The Gray Zone, #3

Other Books:

Outlaw Heartstrings
Sidetracked Love
Only For You
Hard Focus
Salvaged Parts
Spark of the Lock
Dirty Bitches MC: Season 3

More information available at **mldemora.com**.

www.ingramcontent.com/pod-product-compliance
Lightning Source LLC
Chambersburg PA
CBHW070507200726
48293CB00007B/2422